Dead Fish Wind

Dead Fish Wind

By Cooper Levey-Baker

Lake Dallas, Texas

FIRST EDITION

Dead Fish Wind is a work of fiction. Names, characters, places, and incidents either are the products of the author's imagination or are used fictitiously. Any resemblance to actual events, locales, businesses, companies, or persons, living or dead, is entirely coincidental.

Requests for permission to reprint material from this work should be sent to:

Permissions
Madville Publishing
P.O. Box 358
Lake Dallas, TX 75065

Author Photograph: Karen Arango
Cover Design: Gigi Ortwein

ISBN: 978-1-948692-74-8 paperback; 978-1-948692-75-5 ebook
Library of Congress Control Number: 2021940751

To Rachél

Part One

1.

Dead fish had been washing up on the beach off and on for years, but Cicely had never seen anything like this: dead fish everywhere. The bodies floated in on the crests of the gulf's small, foam-filled waves and piled up along the water's edge. Mucus bubbled up between the fish's gills as the waves knocked the corpses farther and farther up the beach, leaving them to bake in the punishing sunshine. Cicely could see the final limp kicks of the few fish still living, twisting in pain. As the final holdouts dropped from this life, one by one, the stacks of fish grew still.

The air stung. It felt like Cicely's eyes were being rubbed with sandpaper. Her whole face grew wet with tears. The stench from the dead fish crawled up inside her and scratched.

Up and down the beach, people fled. Teenagers squeezed their noses shut as they packed up their coolers and towels and bolted for the parking lot. A gray-haired woman launched a hacking cough as she waddled away from the water.

Cicely wanted to stay, wanted to reread her mother's letter again, but every line became a blurry mess. She slipped the pages back into the envelope in which it came, the envelope her mother had addressed to her at work. Cicely hadn't seen or spoken to her in more than a decade—how had she known where she worked? The city in the upper left hand corner, Orlando, at least gave Cicely something to go by, a place to write to. But the PO box told her that her mother didn't want her to find her. Or maybe she just didn't want Cicely's father to find her.

She folded the envelope in half and squeezed it into the back left pocket of her jeans. Sand clung to her legs as she ambled between the dunes, back to the path that wound through the mangroves that clustered between the beach and the bridge, the bridge near home. She wiped the tears from her face with the sleeve of her green men's button-down shirt. What would she tell her father she had been doing down at the beach? It wasn't like her to slip away without telling him. She couldn't mention the letter—he would insist on reading it. But it was hers; it belonged to her.

The mangroves offered respite from the ludicrous heat. A hush fell as she traced the path among their shadows. Kids sneaked back here to have sex, and every now and then she saw an empty beer bottle or a discarded condom sunk into the wet sand. Back here, away from the beach, closer to the bay side of the island, she could still smell the dead fish, but the stench wasn't as sharp. Her path cut underneath the bridge that connected the Circle to the island to the north, where she and her father lived.

What did her mother look like? Cicely had no photos of her—those had all been lost the last time she and her father had been evicted—but Cicely could still summon the details of one taken in their old backyard. In that shot, her mother rested in a tire swing, her feet dangling down almost all the way to neat, freshly chopped grass. The high, curled blond hair, the freckled cheeks, the big shoulders—Cicely remembered all that. But her expression? Was her mother smiling in that photo? Cicely did not know.

She stepped over the battered-down No Trespassing fence that circled her lot. The home stood two stories tall, unfinished and still wrapped in plastic, with hollow spots for doors and windows. The man downtown who owned the property was known to his tenants simply as the Owner. According to the story Cicely heard, when everything collapsed, he bought up all the abandoned half-built homes in the area and started illegally renting them out. Cicely's friend Delanna—who also rented from the Owner—had once pointed out the skyscraper that was supposedly his, but neither of them had ever seen him.

Cicely dealt only with one of his lieutenants, known for his red bandanna and the baby blue box cutter he wore in his belt. He drove around to all the homes at the start of each month to collect the rent.

The rent. The surprise of her mother's letter had made her forget about it. Cicely's father lived with her, but she alone paid their way. For a couple years, Cicely never missed a payment, but last month she caught strep throat and the walk-in clinic had sucked up most of her savings. Now she owed for last month, plus this month, plus interest—almost a thousand dollars. She had no clue how she'd get the cash in the next ten days, before the man with the box cutter was due to drop in again, and she didn't know what to expect if she couldn't come up with the loot. Delanna told her tales about what happened to tenants in arrears. First, they paid interest. Then, if they still couldn't pay, it wasn't enough to just kick them out—they were beaten bloody and told to leave town.

Cicely entered the house through the hole where the double doors were supposed to hang. The room that was intended to be the parlor sat mostly bare. The foundation had been covered only halfway with tile, but Cicely had stolen a tarp from a nearby construction site and used it to cover the bare concrete, weighing it down at each corner with bricks, also stolen. The only furniture were their two chairs, empty. Cicely was perplexed. Had her father actually gone to the VFW to see if someone there might help them with the rent? Cicely had asked him to do so several times, but he never agreed. She felt a surge of relief. She didn't have to hide the letter from him, for now, and maybe, for the first time in years, it wouldn't be on her to find a solution to their problems.

In the bathroom, Cicely splashed water from a bucket onto her face. Even inside the house she could smell the dead fish from the beach, but the pain in her eyes had subsided and her throat no longer itched. She poured a glass of water from another bucket and gulped it down. She checked her watch. She needed to go to work.

2.

The sun was dissolving into pink evening stripes by the time she stepped off the bus, and her shadow stretched way out in front of her, tickling the pitted pavement of the parking lot that sprawled between her and the dance hall where she worked. Built decades ago, the hall predated the retention pond that flanked it, not to mention the Interstate that passed by just to the east. It had once been surrounded by pines and dwarf oaks, but all that was gone now. Back when the hall was built, this area was a separate town from the downtown near the beach, but over the years the county slashed more and more east-west corridors into the woods, and then the Interstate replaced the train tracks, and in what felt like an instant the two town centers bled out toward each other, forming one long, low, concrete mass of subdivisions and shopping centers. The hall—once the site of sock hops, Easter picnics, political rallies—lost the town center it served, and was shuttered for decades. But an investor, the son of a former mayor, had come along a few years ago and restored it. The venue became an instant hit—part concert hall, part city hall, part titty bar, part rec center. Everyone went there, and everything happened there—bake sales, handshake deals, burlesque shows. The same investor who spruced up the hall also paid to construct the towering sign that Cicely now walked toward—a neon-animated outline of a woman lifting up her skirt, with a bright red tongue flashing between her legs.

The bouncer nodded as she walked in the back door. Inside,

she heard the music of the evening's first act—soft and dreamy, a muffled digital beat submerged beneath warm synthesizers and arpeggiated guitar chords. A female singer cooed. The music was fuzzy; it seemed to crawl through the hall, poking into corners and settling into the grooves of the walls and rafters. It wasn't loud, but it filled space.

Cicely poked her head out through one of the side curtains. The singer's face was unfamiliar. Her dress looked like it was made out of a thousand pearl coins, and it rattled when she shook her hips.

The stage had been built for the big brass bands popular decades ago, and it dwarfed the singer, who was backed by a tight tuxedo-clad trio. Lights hanging from the ceiling filled the air with a woozy blue light. Only a few of the tables at the foot of the stage were full—it was early still. A pair of servers, each of them topless, dressed in nothing but black, low-slung tights and heels, brought Mai Tais, the house cocktail, to the men sitting up close. The men stared at the singer, transfixed. One mouthed the words she was singing. Like the singer's face, the faces down front were unfamiliar to Cicely. Had the singer brought them out? Did they know her from some other venue?

Cicely walked back to the dressing room, where she found Delanna, who started as a server on the same day as Cicely a few years back, and Hilda, another server. Delanna nodded when Cicely came in; she was in the middle of telling Hilda a story about her boyfriend.

"… been hurting him for weeks, so he finally goes to the doctor. The doctor says it's clogged up and needs to get cleaned out. This assistant comes in with this little water sprayer and starts shooting it into his ear." Delanna leaned into her mirror and streaked her eyelashes with mascara. "So he's already freaking out, because he says it feels like his brain is getting soaked, when, no joke, the assistant looks down in the bowl where all this gunk from his ear is collecting and sees this little worm-thing, this parasite, wiggling." Delanna rubbed the edge of her eyes with a pinkie and laughed. "So she starts freaking out. He's freaking out. God what a scene." She twisted her mascara brush back into its tube.

"So what was it?" Hilda asked. Still new to the job, Hilda always arrived a half-hour early and was ready for her shift well before everyone else. She had already taken off her top. Her breasts curved outward; the nipples pointed away from her body. Delanna's, meanwhile, sat upright. Her areolae stared at Cicely.

Delanna shrugged. "They wanted to do a follow-up, but we can't afford that."

Hilda shook her head—"Fucked up," she said—and walked out the door, down the hallway that led to the hall floor. Now that the sun was setting, the venue would start filling up with the customers the women were happiest to see—the businessmen and politicians entertaining clients and benefactors. They tipped too much and drove up prices for the rest of the room.

Cicely wiggled out of her jeans and grabbed a pair of black tights from a rack loaded with them. "Those stories about being late with the Owner, that's bullshit, right?" The gentle murmur of the singer floated through the walls.

Delanna was putting on lipstick. "I hear bad things."

Cicely hopped up and down to get the tights over her hips. As she picked up her jeans from the floor, her mother's letter fell out of the back pocket. She hid it in her cubby before Delanna could ask. "Every month," Cicely said, "it just feels like I can never catch up." She never talked money with Delanna, had never told her much about her father, but desperation made bringing up the topic less awkward. She had taken the job at the dance hall thinking it would pay well, but it never did. Her father—if only he would help. The honest part of her told her she was stupid for thinking he might have actually gone to the VFW today. He probably spent the day wasting what little money she had managed to save. Cicely slumped into a chair and started doing her makeup, too. If Delanna heard what Cicely said, she didn't show it.

The song onstage came to an end. Sparse but enthusiastic

applause burst out. Someone turned on the house music. The singer brushed into the dressing room, out of breath and covered in sweat. She guzzled a glass of water and slipped the straps of her tight dress from her shoulders. Even without the straps, the dress gripped her lithe body. The singer stood a head taller than Cicely, with a bush of curly silver hair that shot out from her scalp, but she wasn't old—maybe thirty, Cicely guessed. Her wrists looked delicate, but her upper arms swelled with a toned heft. As the singer kicked off her heels, Cicely caught a glimpse of the fine hairs that had just begun to show on her thighs. The singer downed a second glass of water and wiped her lips with the back of her hand. She unleashed a pent-up sigh.

Delanna stood up. "Nice show."

The singer reached out and cupped Delanna's right breast. "You too." Her voice offstage sounded deep and beaten, so unlike the feathery sound she projected with her band. She had an accent, too, something glottalic, but Cicely couldn't place it. Goosebumps rose along Cicely's forearms. Who was this stranger?

The singer took her hand from Delanna's breast and turned to Cicely. "You?"

Cicely looked down at her own chest. She was still wearing her green men's shirt.

"I don't think they'll let you out there like that," the singer said. She turned her back to Cicely and Delanna and began to wiggle out of her dress, which fit so tightly the top seam left a bright red horizontal line along her back, just below her shoulder blades. She wasn't wearing a bra, just white panties, and when she turned around, Cicely could see her dark nest of pubic hair through the fabric. A faint scar cut vertically up her side, just above the elastic waist of her underwear. Cicely looked from the scar to the singer's eyes, which had been watching her.

Delanna opened her eyes wide and looked back and forth from Cicely to the singer. "Fucking weirdos," she said, turning to leave.

Cicely hurried after Delanna, unbuttoning her shirt as she

walked down the hallway and out to the floor. Before the door to the dressing room closed behind her, she looked back one last time. The singer was lighting a cigarette, staring right at her, as the door closed from left to right, disappearing her inch by inch—arm, bosom, chin, neck, shoulder, arm—till it landed in its frame with a thud. A puff of the singer's smoke hung in front of the closed door for a moment, then dispersed.

And then the men began calling for their Mai Tais, and Cicely's shift began.

The crowd stood up for the evening's main act, a reggae cover band. Some danced; most simply talked more loudly. A customer spilled sticky liquor down Cicely's back. The bouncer threw out three men: two had started fighting and the third was recording the scene with his cell phone.

The air-conditioning kept the hall frigid and dry, and by the end of the night Cicely's nipples were so sore they felt bruised. She shivered as she walked back to the dressing room to put on her shirt and jeans. The singer had vanished. Did any of the other girls know her? She'd ask tomorrow. Now, like always at the end of a shift, she just wanted out.

After changing, she counted the night's money: forty bucks, minus the ten the hall deducted for the two Styrofoam containers of food she brought home. Her haul was paltry compared to Delanna's. Cicely just pretended to be friendly with the customers; Delanna actually cared about her tables having a good time, pausing to flirt with the rich old guys and sitting in their laps if they begged enough. Did she feel their erections? The thought made Cicely shudder. She slipped her thirty remaining dollars into the envelope with her mother's letter and stepped from the dressing room out into the hot, clammy night, hoping the bus driver wouldn't be playing a movie. But her heart sank when she saw the idling bus. Light from the TV on board strobed out into the street. The screen was so big, so violently colorful, and the driver had cranked the sound up so high she could already hear the jokes and the farting noises as she walked across the parking lot. She had already seen parts of tonight's movie—*Famous Anus*—on previous trips. Through the windows of the bus, she could see passengers laughing uproariously. She stepped up into the vehicle, crestfallen, almost unable to bear the prospect of having to endure the ride home.

The bus—its few remaining passengers still chuckling at the movie—dropped her off at the foot of the bridge that arched from downtown to the Circle. A gust of dead fish smell hit her in the face. The wind blew strong enough to bend the palm trees in half, and with each whip of air, she coughed a little. Out by the hall, where the smell had not yet reached, she had forgotten about what she had seen on the beach that morning.

Over the bridge, traffic light this late, her thoughts returned to the rent. Tonight's earnings, combined with the little she had been able to save here and there, added up to maybe five hundred. But even that would only catch them up to last month. What about this month? And next? She didn't want to think anymore. She leaned into the breeze as she walked over the bridge, around the Circle, across the second bridge, and home. Inside, the wind was just a soft echo.

There he sat: her father, in his chair, sucking on his pipe and gurgling smoke into the air above him. The orange orb of the pipe glowed. Although his muscles had withered in recent years, he would always look strong to Cicely, who still remembered his sinewy arms and thick thighs, the effortlessness with which he lifted her up. Sitting in his chair, now, he didn't look relaxed, but coiled. He didn't acknowledge her. She didn't want to hear the truth right away, so she left the food on the floor and walked past him to the bathroom, where she splashed her face with water from bucket number one and tried to make out her features in the mirror. Her plucked eyebrows stood out against the soft milky blue of her forehead; her eyes were dark hollows. It was like being buried alive, slowly, this life—lying there in a box cut into the loam, face up, as clump after clump of dirt slips down on you, first just on your clothes, maybe a little inside your shoes, then suddenly tickling your elbows, and before you know it, it's pressing down a bit on your stomach, coming together under your chin, the weight growing deeper and deeper, the feeling like being pulled down into the earth—not being covered, but being sucked in, strangled from below. Was there anything left? The face in the mirror showed her nothing.

She walked back into the parlor. Her father had opened one of the Styrofoam containers and was sucking on a chicken wing. "Any luck today?" she asked, drying her hands on her jeans. "Any luck with your friends?" Although on the surface she always hoped for deliverance, there was a part of Cicely, often hidden even from herself, that found pleasure in bad news. A portion of her looked forward to disappointment, as if it were confirmation of the essential rottenness of everything around her.

Her father gnawed at a little knob of chicken meat. His pipe sat on the right arm of his chair, still glowing. In the distance, Cicely could hear sirens, a boat revving, the plastic on the outside of the house flapping in the wind.

"No luck?"

Slurp.

"Christ, I knew you wouldn't even go." She kicked his chair.

He glared at her. His face carried deep lines along his forehead and around his cheeks. Even as a young man, he had looked old. When Cicely was a kid, her mother said that the furnace at the factory had baked him like a piece of clay, and that his face had started cracking. When she was little, Cicely thought her mother was being playful, affectionate, by saying that, but now Cicely realized what she really meant.

He spit out the bone of his chicken wing onto the tarp underfoot. His eyes regarded her. You're a stranger, they said.

Cicely turned from him. "I give up. You can go live in a ditch. I'm going to bed."

She climbed up into the dark of the second story, feeling her way along the wall to where she kept her mattress, a pale, lumpy thing. Normally, she just tucked her money away underneath the bed, but her father's eyes left her cold and scared. She collected what she had already saved from beneath the mattress and put that in the envelope with tonight's money, taking out her mother's letter in the process. Long before she and her father moved in, thieves had stripped the walls of all its copper. Cicely now located one of the holes they had bashed open to get at the metal and slipped the envelope stuffed with money inside a slit in a puffy sheet of insulation. She had never told anyone—even her father—about that hiding spot.

She plopped down on the mattress, pulling a grungy sweatshirt over her like a blanket. Once her eyes adjusted, the midnight blue light reflecting up from the water and filtering though the house was just bright enough for her to make out words on paper. She lay on her back with one hand behind her head and read through her mother's letter in full for a second time.

> *C.,*
>
> *Monday was garbage day, which meant Sunday was garbage day, because that was the day when I had to put the stuff out.*
>
> *Bath nights were Monday and Thursday.*
>
> *Of course every night I made dinner for the three of us, which meant going shopping with you during the day, running errands to different stores, hauling you in and out.*
>
> *I loaded the dishwasher and scrubbed the big dishes by hand and unloaded the dishes when the machine was done, scrubbing by hand those that hadn't gotten clean in the machine.*
>
> *I made coffee every morning.*
>
> *I brought in the mail every evening.*
>
> *Tuesday was laundry day.*
>
> *Wednesday was the other garbage day, the day I had to put out the lawn clippings and pine straw and leaves, which first had to be bagged up.*
>
> *Coming from me, after so long, this letter will probably seem strange. But as I sit down and think about the years I spent raising you, the memories that come back to me first are the chores.*

Before I moved in with your father, I always thought of a home as something static, a place with walls and a roof and things inside that didn't move. I was wrong.
    M.

Cicely pressed the paper to her chest and cried. The letter left her furious but also tenderhearted—angry at her mother's memories, warmed by the thought that her mother had any memories of her at all. When Cicely's sobs ebbed, she hid the letter under her mattress and rolled over. Falling asleep felt like being sucked backward into the warm, dry mouth of a giant lizard.

3.

The singer's name was Zinnia—a floral name, like Cicely. Absurd, being named for a flower in a place where flowers wouldn't grow without phosphoric acid and potassium chloride.

Day by day, the crowd for Zinnia's shows at the hall expanded, with faces none of the girls had seen before. They were all men, and they all came alone, wearing jean jackets with the sleeves cut off, camouflage baseball caps, puffy fishing vests. They stared up at the stage as if entranced. When Zinnia's set ended, the men quickly paid their bills, tipped well, and departed. They didn't seem to know one another, and they never conversed.

Cicely introduced herself to Zinnia on the singer's fourth night. She was unable to get much out besides her name. She didn't understand why Zinnia intimidated her so much. Delanna wasn't impressed. She just figured Zinnia was another song-and-dance chick who would flake out any day. The dance hall had seen plenty of them, young women with good voices who were able to build a small local rep out of a few good covers, a tight dress, and some pouty lips, but who inevitably faded after a couple weeks, when it became clear they had nothing more to offer. The cycle was predictable: the singers would start staying late after their sets, pounding Mai Tais with the busboys, next they'd be passing out drunk in the bathroom and waking up when the cleaning lady came in around noon. Zinnia seemed too in-control for that fate, though, and her audience was devoted in a way Cicely had never seen before.

"Where did you used to sing?" Cicely asked one night after Zinnia's set was over. Cicely was on break, watching the singer pack away her sparkly dress, which never seemed to lose its luster.

Zinnia zipped up the garment bag that held her dress and pulled her cigarette from her lips. She exhaled. "Around." She pulled a white men's dress shirt down over her torso; it was the only shirt she ever wore, and she never bothered to even unbutton it. She put on a pair of jeans. Her expression seemed dismissive to Cicely, disinterested, but not unfriendly. Perhaps she liked for people to pry.

Cicely tried a compliment: "You have so many fans."

Zinnia leaned her head back and stared up. Cicely could see the soft line under her chin where her makeup ended and her plain flesh began. In the dress shirt, she looked masculine, breast-less, so unlike her image onstage. "I dabble," she said to the ceiling. Her white shirt was yellow around the collar; small coffee stains dotted the chest. Cicely stared at the little hollow where Zinnia's clavicles came together. Zinnia lowered her gaze. "Got to go." She picked up the book bag she always came to the hall with and slung it over her shoulder. "Need a ride?"

The door to the parking lot was open and almost closed before Cicely snapped out of her trance and stopped the door from shutting with her foot. "Got a couple more hours," she shouted to Zinnia, who was already halfway across the lot.

Zinnia climbed into a massive blue van, the decades-old kind that had one of those sliding doors you had to wind up and slam to shut and actual flower-print curtains inside the windows. Starting up, the engine sounded like a broken lawnmower. The van rattled and shook. Zinnia rolled down her window. "Rain check then," she shouted over the noise.

"How can she afford a car?" Cicely asked Delanna after walking back out onto the hall floor. The crowd was light. Some big football game was happening; the regulars were all off drinking somewhere else.

Delanna snorted: "More like a tractor."

"She can't make much here."

Delanna turned to her with a surprised look. "Why are you so curious about her?" Her mouth made a malicious smile.

Cicely saw that it delighted Delanna to catch a glimpse of her thoughts. It was stupid of her to be candid. She shrugged.

The rest of the night was one of those slow nights when Cicely didn't even mind not making much money, although the entertainment—an interpretative dance performance of last year's hit comedy *Testes Testes One Two Three*—was terrible. Cicely never felt as alone as she did when people around her laughed. Was she boring? Or did people like stupid shit? Maybe both. She knew she wasn't interesting. When her father lost his job, she dropped out of high school and found work. Her mother abandoning her had already made her a serious kid; having to care for her father robbed her of anything lighthearted. But even that didn't explain how alone she felt when she heard coworkers talk about the movies and TV shows they watched, or when they showed her funny videos on their phones. Cicely always thought she was missing something, that maybe if the others explained what was so funny, she might understand, but explanations only confused her more—what was so funny about that man being struck in the groin with a baseball bat? Eventually, people just stopped sharing things. She passed from feeling alone to feeling alone.

Even her father barely spoke to her, but it hadn't always been that way. When Cicely first found the house by the beach, they stayed up late and played gin rummy in the moonlight, and if Cicely had some cash in her pocket she'd run to the store to grab a case of cheap beer. Their conversation consisted of bullshit—they never spoke about Cicely's mother—but at least Cicely felt like here was an actual human being with whom she was sharing a moment that could not be taken from her and she was happy and this other person seemed happy, too. Now she didn't even have that.

The night made her so mopey she almost missed the bus, but luckily the TV on the bus had broken, and the ride home was silent. Cicely felt so down she didn't even fret about the rent, still looming, still due in a few days. Whatever would happen would happen, and there was little use caring one way or the other. Even the prospect of being bloodied barely registered. She would have as much money as she could earn, and if that wasn't enough, then she and her father would have to leave. They would scurry somewhere else, find a roof, and start the process all over again.

Cicely rested her forehead against the window and stared. Outside, the city was quiet. Except for the hall, the whole town shut down pretty early. People were making runs to 7-Eleven; there wasn't much else to do. Inside the bus, the air-conditioning was jacked up so high that the windows started to fog. When Cicely pulled back her head, the whole window was cloudy, except for the oval where her skin had been.

4.

Cicely didn't work on Tuesdays, so she and her father had made a habit of walking together to the field just south of downtown where volunteers from St. Mark's Church showed a sermon and served lunch to the poor each week. Cicely put on her only dress, a pale yellow A-line with pockets, and her father wore the checkered gray shirt and red tie she washed for him each week. Everyone else tried to dress up for the event, too, and if you stood far enough away from the crowd you might mistake the gathering for just another ice cream social, but up close the details revealed need: tan pants with holes in back pockets, mismatched buttons on threadbare suits, shoes with flapping soles.

The field itself sloped down toward a high stage, where the St. Mark's parishioners had erected a massive screen that seemed too bright even in the middle of the day. The liver-spotted face of Father Bill loomed over the crowd, and speakers carried his sibilant recitations to the furthest edges of the grass, where stood Port-a-Potties emblazoned with the church's seal. The crowd had grown so large in recent years that the police began stopping traffic on the road that curved around the property. The audience on this Tuesday looked even bigger than usual. Cicely guessed it was because the fish had everyone spooked.

"... give first so that it may be given to us," Father Bill was saying. "Now what do I mean by that?"

Rumors that Father Bill wasn't even local had been circulating for years. No one Cicely knew had ever seen him in the flesh.

"Give what?" Father Bill asked. "In these times of woe,

when we're all struggling mightily simply to live with dignity, what more can we give?"

Standing beside her father on the outskirts of the crowd, Cicely couldn't help thinking that he looked handsome, and that it was because of her. Early in the morning, she set the washing bucket out in the sun to warm the water so she could lather his face with soap and shave him. You could see small nicks if you knew to look for them, but she had done the best she could. He appeared decent. His face was pale where his whiskers had been, a contrast with his red cheeks and the scalp touched pink by the sun that was visible through his thin, wintery hair. He was just as drawn into himself in public as he was at home, but here his posture straightened and he held his head up. The coldness she saw in his eyes the night she kicked his chair had vaporized, leaving his face bemused. He stood listening to Father Bill with his hands clasped behind his back, chewing his lower lip and listening respectfully. Did he believe in God? He was raised Episcopal, but he had never mentioned the Lord's name in her presence, except to curse.

"But listen to Luke 6:38, and when I say listen, I mean it. Listen." Father Bill emphasized each syllable: "'Give, and it shall be given unto you.' Do you hear that? Do you feel the power of those words? The truth? 'A good portion will fall into your lap. The portion you give will determine the portion you receive in return.'"

A small cheer went up from the most fervent believers, those who clustered near the screen. Up close, so big, Father Bill's face must have looked like the face of God. Cicely noticed that someone had vandalized the enormous banner that hung above the screen. It now read St. Marx.

"Sounds good doesn't it?" Father Bill paused. "Sounds good to me. It sounds very good, very good. And this promise that God has made—that whatever you give will be repaid to you—is no idle promise, nothing like those promises we keep hearing from Washington, DC." Scattered boos. "No. No, no. God never makes a promise he won't keep. I promise you that." Father Bill put on his pensive face. "Now, before we join together in prayer to bless our meal, I'd like to read you another passage, this one from Mark, the book of Mark, Mark 11:24. 'Therefore I say to you, whatever you pray and ask for, believe that you will receive it, and it will be so for you.'" Father Bill looked as if he were fighting back tears. "Whatever you pray and ask for, it will be so. It will be so. It will be so."

Shouts of "Hallelujah!" and "Amen!" rang out from the crowd. As Cicely bent to scratch at a small cluster of mosquito bites on her ankle, her stomach rumbled. From behind each side of the giant screen, St. Mark's volunteers—recognizable from their flowing red robes—walked down into the crowd, bearing offering plates lined with red felt. The golden rims glimmered in the sun.

Cicely's father spat on the ground.

"Papa?"

He turned to her. "I hate accepting food from these people."

It wouldn't stop him from eating it, Cicely knew. But she tempered her annoyance. "No worse than me taking food from work."

Cicely watched as a teenage boy pulled a dollar bill from his New Balances and placed it in one of the offering plates. A young, red-robed woman holding one of the golden discs started to walk toward Cicely and her father, but her father's sneer made the volunteer stop short. She turned back toward the condensed center of the audience.

Once the offering had been collected, the volunteers pulled the tops off the chafing dishes lined up on office tables to the left of the screen. Cicely was starving, but didn't protest when her father cut in front of her in line. When no one was looking, she snatched a whole handful of plastic spoons from the napkin-lined basket at the end of the buffet. You never knew.

The food was always simple—beef stews, lentil soups, dry biscuits—but today's meal was the most basic yet: just a bowl of plain white unseasoned grits with a ladle of tomato sauce on top. There were no tables at which to eat, so Cicely and her father sat cross-legged in the grass, brown and crushed from so many feet trampling on it. The mosquito bites on Cicely's ankle required another vigorous scratch.

Despite their simplicity, the Tuesday meals put most people in a good mood, and Cicely enjoyed watching people mill about, eating and talking. She smiled at anyone who looked her in the eye. She would have liked to start a conversation with someone, but no one ever came close enough. Her father slurped up his food as quickly as possible so he could get back in line before the others. In his haste, a drop of maroon tomato sauce dripped from his spoon and onto his tan pants. He didn't even notice. He had looked handsome to Cicely before; now he looked like an animal again, an ape. Was this what her mother had seen before she left? The few photos Cicely had seen of her father when he was young made him look almost refined. In one, he stood next to five or six guys in gray boiler suits at the factory, but he himself was dressed in blue jeans and a spotless, bright white V-neck T-shirt, the cuffs of his pants rolled up above shiny black loafers. The men in boiler suits glared at the camera with hatred; Cicely's father beamed. He looked like the guy in the group that the other guys would call "gay."

As lunch wound down, all those gathered in the field began talking about the piles of dead fish. Everyone had a theory. Tallahassee was behind it, punishing the city because the governor was feuding with the mayor. Or it must be leftover residue from one of last year's oil spills, seeping up out of the gulf floor and killing the fish. Or it had to be related to that golf course they were rehabbing out east, the one they were using all the orange chemicals on. And what was up with all those helicopters buzzing the other day? Was that related to the catastrophe? No one in this crowd knew anything. Cicely herself hadn't been down to the beach since that first day, but the stench had hung around, strengthening and weakening depending on the tides and the direction of the wind.

"I wonder what Father Bill makes of all the dead fish," she said to her father.

He snorted into his second helping of grits. "You of all people—"

"I was joking, Papa."

He looked up. "Right."

Monday was garbage day. But Sunday was really garbage day. Was that how it went?

"Papa, I really do need you to go to the VFW tomorrow." She shooed flies away from her bowl, even though she had finished eating. "Really. Can you do that?"

He stood up, stretched his arms up high. Sweat had seeped through the armpits of his shirt. He crumpled his plastic bowl in half. "I'll think about it."

The crowd was beginning to break apart, some slogging back onto the road, back north, toward the bus depot, while others walked east to catch the buses that would take them out near the Interstate. The St. Mark's volunteers, their red robes now heavy and damp with perspiration, began hosing out the chafing dishes. They lowered a plastic sheet over the screen to protect it from rain. Cicely threw her bowl in the green dumpster next to the toilets. She scratched her ankle for a third time. Her fingertips came up bloody.

5.

Zinnia was smoking in her van when Cicely got off work the next night. She motioned Cicely over and asked if she wanted to go for a ride. Cicely jumped inside.

Sable Ranch, Heritage Harbor, Poinsettia Point, Oak Preserve, the Village at Windermere, Plantation Trace, Fox Glen Acres ... gated community after gated community flew through the window. They were heading north. Cicely stared at the lit-up signage, the crisply arranged bougainvilleas and sea grapes, the brick guardhouses and electric gates, the smooth black roads that led back into the neighborhoods themselves. The night air was foggy and damp. Cicely turned from the window and watched Zinnia drive; the horrible buzz of the van's engine made conversation impossible. Zinnia gripped the steering wheel at ten and two and never took her eyes off the road. The cigarette between her lips burned down to the filter before she spat it out onto the floor.

All the seats in the back of the van had been removed. A white cooler the size of a coffin sat strapped to the left side. Glass bottles rattled about on the grooved metal floor as Zinnia turned westward, out toward the last remaining fishing village on the coast, where the streets ran narrow and out-of-work fishermen lolled about all night. The homes out here were really just trailers jacked up on cinder blocks so they could ride out floods.

Zinnia parked at the foot of a small bridge that connected the village to the islands, grabbed a bottle from the rear of the van, and started walking toward the bridge master's tower that stood halfway across the span. Cicely followed her up a short flight of stairs and into the tower's one small, glassed-in room. When Cicely got there, Zinnia was fiddling in a mini-fridge.

"Looking for tonic," Zinnia said, shaking the half-drunk bottle of gin she had taken from the van.

Through the glass, Cicely could see the towers of light emanating from the ritziest condos on the islands.

"Ah-ha!" Zinnia twisted the cap off a small plastic bottle. It hissed.

Cicely sat on a green canvas cot while Zinnia poured drinks into doubled-up paper cups. "Is this where you live?"

Snort. "I just like to come up here sometimes. Nobody uses it anymore."

Cicely looked around the cramped room. Indeed, it looked as if it hadn't been used in years. Spiders had drawn a dense web over the drawbridge control panel and grime jammed the edges of the windows.

"It's just a place to be," Zinnia said, looking uncomfortable for the first time Cicely could remember. She fidgeted with her cup.

"Cheers," Cicely said, raising her cup. She gagged when she drank—it was three-quarters gin.

"Take her easy now."

"I wish I had someplace like this—with windows."

"Delanna told me you live in one of the Owner's places."

Cicely nodded and looked into her cup. A fly landed on its rim. "I wish we didn't." She drank, the gin not so surprising this time.

"We?"

"My father." Cicely looked into Zinnia's face. Her eyes were the color of palm fronds, her forehead smooth and unwrinkled. A slight shadow seemed to coat her upper lip, and her silvery hair, pulled back tight, fell loose around her ears. Offstage, she was pretty, not beautiful. Zinnia leaned back against a window.

Cicely sucked down the last bit of her drink. "Where did you learn to sing?" She held out her cup for a refill.

"It's my turn to say, 'My father.'" Zinnia poured them each another round then sat down beside Cicely. "My dad was always banging on a piano. He used to make me and my sister stand at attention while he played chords and we had to mimic the sound. He traveled to Europe, performed over there, played with Ornette Coleman." Zinnia's weight on the cot made Cicely lean toward her. "He could play the piano, but he was a fucking loser. He could never stick with anything long enough to do anything worth anything. But he taught me and my sister to sing, I'll give him that." Zinnia's shoulder touched Cicely's. "I actually went to college to study music, but I got kicked out halfway through. A girl I knew got stabbed." She laughed. "By me."

"What did she do?"

"Ha. Most people, when I tell them that, they ask why I did it. That's what Delanna asked."

Cicely felt her face go hot. Her jealousy surprised her.

"But not you," Zinnia said, chuckling. "You know that if I stabbed someone I must have had a good reason."

The tension inside Cicely eased; she felt like she had passed a test.

"I was paying my way through school selling weed," Zinnia said. "And this one girl who hated me because I fucked her boyfriend found out and told the provost. So I whittled a drumstick and stabbed her in the thigh while she was waiting in line in the lunchroom. I was going to get kicked out anyway. Why not?"

Cicely's mind skipped right over the stabbing and back to the rent. "Is that how you can afford your van?"

"Weed? Pffft. I wish. Can't get my hands on any these days."

Cicely felt stupid, like she always did when she hoped. It wasn't worth the pain. Her first job after dropping out of school had been at an A&W, frying fries and mixing milkshakes for customers she despised. The air in the kitchen didn't just stink— it actually felt greasy, like you could sense the fat floating around, accumulating on your skin, clump by clump, and sticking in the threads of your hair. This was back when she and her father still had their original home, the one her mother had left them to, with its running water and hot showers and everything, and each night after a shift at A&W she would scrub and scrub at her dark hair till it felt slick and clean, but even then, after all that cleaning, when she would wake in the morning she would see a small clot of grease left behind on the pillow, as if she was marked for life, as if the A&W would never let her go.

But the A&W only paid minimum wage, and after a couple years, around when she turned eighteen, after the umpteenth notice of foreclosure from the bank, she was finally able to find what she thought would be a better job, tending the buffet at a Ponderosa. No more deep fryer, no more microwave duty— this time she was out in the restaurant, breathing the air that regular people breathed. At the time, it felt like a breakthrough, but Cicely now bitterly remembered this time of optimism, those months she arranged curly parsley and refilled steak drawers and earned enough to mostly cover the bills at the small apartment she and her father had moved into, where the rent was due each week.

She felt sorry for her father during those years, and with him hated her mother—blaming her for leaving them, blaming her for how everything had collapsed around them. Her father just needed a few years to regroup, she told herself as she served old ladies who weren't strong enough to lift the spoon that sat in the tray of mashed potatoes. He'll get bored, she thought as she bussed tables and clapped ashtrays together over garbage bins. He'll get back on his feet.

"Can you play any instruments?" Zinnia asked. She split the last of the gin and tonic between her cup and Cicely's.

Cicely shook her head.

Zinnia pointed at a dusty black case in the corner. "A guy who used to play in the band loaned me a zither and then never came back to pick it up."

Cicely didn't even know what a zither was. She was listening to Zinnia but not really paying attention. Whenever her mind turned to the Ponderosa, it inevitably settled on that one day, a couple years after she started, when the owner introduced Mike, the new manager, and he had given her that sick grin underneath that foul mustache, and then her memory tripped back to that day a couple weeks later, when Mike called her to his office and took off his belt. Cicely squeezed her eyes shut.

Zinnia plucked at the zither. Its high-pitched notes quivered in the air. She wasn't making music, just trying out the strings. She must have noticed Cicely's emotion, but she ignored it. Cicely felt grateful. She sniffled and wiped her nose with the little knob of flesh between her thumb and forefinger.

"So how do you afford your van?" Cicely finally asked.

Zinnia stood in the middle of the room and swayed slightly, clutching the zither to her chest. Through the window, Cicely saw the drawbridge slowly crank open. A yacht glided through. She could hear the loud chatter of a party coming from the boat. The fog outside had mostly lifted.

Zinnia hummed a few bars of a tune Cicely didn't recognize and strummed a minor chord. She softly sang her response: "Can you keep a secret?"

6.

Another letter from Cicely's mother arrived at the dance hall. Two letters, a week apart, after a decade of nothing.

During her first fifteen-minute break, Cicely sat down in the dressing room and examined the envelope: the Orlando PO box in the upper left corner matched the address on the first envelope. She ripped open the paper sleeve. The letter had been written on a computer, just like the first. Even the font was the same.

Her mother's first letter was cryptic, her second only slightly less so.

> C.,
>
> I need to take back one thing I said in my first letter—that all I think of when I think of the years we had together are chores. That's untrue. We had good times. Even when I think of your father, as awful as he became over the years, as lazy and mean as he could get, I still remember when I met him on the beach. He was there with his buddies one day when I was home from college. He looked so handsome and happy. I wish I remember the excuse he made up to come over and talk to me. I wonder if I regret that summer. I guess I do.
>
> Thinking of the beach makes me think of our Sundays. Do you remember those? I loved

packing up our things in the morning in that big straw basket I found at Goodwill. I loved that basket so much I wore it out. One of the handles fell off, but I just looped a short bungee cord through one side to make up for it. No matter how well I cleaned it, it always had little grains of sand tucked into the thin little ropes on the bottom.

My favorite moment each week was when everything had been set up—the umbrella was standing, the towels had been unfurled—and I could just plop down on my stomach and zone out. This one time—I remember it so vividly— this one time I did just that, I flopped down face-first and you—you must have been around ten or so—you thought I had fallen asleep so you started burying me with sand from the feet up. At first, it felt just like a light showering of crystals, but you kept at it and over time it got really dense, really heavy. It must have been summertime, because I remember my back felt like it was burning but I couldn't move because I didn't want to make cracks in the sand around my legs. I didn't want to ruin all your hard work. So I just lay there and listened to you giggle like you were getting away with something. And as my back grew hotter and hotter, the sand kept crawling higher and higher up my legs to the bottom of my swimsuit, and you kept piling it on and on. The sand you dug up felt frigid on my legs, as if you found it on the moon.
M.

Cicely didn't remember that particular afternoon, but she had never forgotten those Sundays. Her mother would slather sunscreen on both of them, careful to reapply after each splash in the water, then she would lie back underneath their umbrella with her book while Cicely would explore, digging up shells and sticking her fingers in the narrow holes dug by the small translucent crabs that skittered back and forth in the foamy water that clung to the sand after the gentle gulf waves rolled back out. Those long summer afternoons, when the sun just seemed to hang there, far out, as if it would never go down.

She crumpled up the letter and threw it in the trash, then sat still and waited till the end of her break, staring at a beige light switch. What did her mother want with these strange messages? Was she trying to explain herself? Why now? Just guilt? Or was she trying to tell Cicely she was out there, waiting for her to find her? Why not just fucking write that then? Cicely had more pressing problems than deciphering ancient and useless memories.

Break ended. As the evening shift dragged, Cicely's anger melted away. When her shift was up and she repaired to the dressing room, she went straight to the trashcan to retrieve her mother's letter, but someone must have emptied it. The letter was lost.

7.

Cicely didn't know what she was driving to the hospital to pick up, but she understood it was likely illegal.

Her first guess: pills. Despite a much-publicized crackdown, they still flooded the city. If you knew the right password you could buy them at most convenience stores, and more than one bartender slung them at the dance hall. But Zinnia had tut-tutted all that: prison sentences for selling pills had grown longer and longer in recent years, and only the well-connected and well-armed could compete in that market.

The van rumbled and shook as Cicely drove. All she knew was that she needed to be below the footbridge at Delphine and Azalea at exactly one a.m. Zinnia's contact, a female nurse who worked the graveyard shift at the hospital, had a ten-minute window in which to drop the item from the bridge, and Cicely had to be right on time to make sure the nurse could drop the package and split. If the nurse was caught with whatever it was she was stealing, they'd be screwed.

Cicely hadn't driven in years. Her parents owned a car back when she was in middle school—before the crash, when owning a car was no big deal for most folks—and her father had taught Cicely to drive before she was old enough to. Zinnia hadn't asked if she had a valid license, and she didn't, so she stayed right around the speed limit and was careful to always use her blinkers. Her heart pumped vigorously. She felt more alert than she had in months. Traffic was sparse, but every so often headlights would flash in the rearview and a car would slip by on the left. The few cars that were out this late were nearly all luxury models. Cicely fretted that the rattling van would draw attention. Zinnia had told her not to worry—she had done many similar runs and had never even seen a cop.

Cicely took a right on Delphine and the hospital rose up to the left. The first E in the sign for the emergency room was blinking. An ambulance with a flat front tire leaned against the sidewalk out front. At the corner of Azalea, Cicely stopped the van and checked the clock. Early by three minutes. She cut the engine and stepped out. Why'd she wear a coat? Getting ready, she had thought it would make her look nondescript, but now she realized how foolish she looked in a jacket when the air was still so dense and hot. With her hands in her pockets, she strolled closer to the footbridge that connected the second stories of the two buildings on either side of the street.

The wind whistled. Back over by the ER, two guys in teal-colored nurse outfits came out to examine the ambulance's flat tire. They muttered to each other, glanced over in Cicely's direction, then went back inside. Over all this, back behind the hospital tower, hung the moon, pink and rotund. The air smelled like pepper.

Footsteps on the bridge—the soft squeak, squeak of tennis shoes. Cicely stepped out of the shadows and into the moonlight. A pink-haired woman in pink scrubs was standing in the middle of the bridge, looking down into the street. When she saw Cicely, she nodded, and Cicely nodded back. Then the nurse placed a green plastic bag big enough to hold a watermelon on the railing of the bridge and waved Cicely closer. The nurse looked left and right and then—coast clear—lifted the bag from the railing and dangled it over the edge. Cicely put her hands in the air and the bag fell and landed in her arms with a sick *squirch*. Cicely recoiled. The package felt dry on the outside, but it slipped in her hands, and she almost dropped it on the pavement.

For a moment, Cicely saw herself from outside her own body. What had she been driven to? But that moment passed, and Cicely felt only one imperative: get out.

She hustled over to the rear of the van. The door clicked open. Up into the van Cicely climbed and down into the cooler fell the bag. Cicely poked at it. *Squirch.* She covered it halfway with ice then shut the cooler's lid. As the van doors slammed closed, relief tickled through her. She was almost gone. As she walked to the driver's side door, she looked back toward the entrance to the ER. The relief she felt vanished. One of the teal-scrubbed nurses was pacing back and forth by the broken-down ambulance, talking on a cell phone. Had he seen her? Fuck, oh fuck. Cicely stepped up into the driver's seat and the engine chugged to life. The nurse looked up. What had he seen? Was he talking to the police right now? Could he see the van's license plate from there? Cicely breathed slowly, told herself she needed to drive away as methodically and legally as she had driven here. She shifted into D and slipped into the side streets that snaked northward. She took random lefts and rights till she was sure nobody was coming after her then exited the neighborhood around the hospital for the main artery that connected up to the fishing village where Zinnia had taken her.

The farther she got from the hospital, the more the anxiety in Cicely's stomach loosened, and her thoughts turned to what was in the cooler. Zinnia had assured her she wasn't picking up anything hazardous, but that didn't explain much. That *squirch* sound. How slippery the bag was. How difficult to grasp. Goosebumps rose from Cicely's forearms. She ran through the possibilities. A sack of kidneys? Lungs? A heart? How could Zinnia make money with any of that? She had fronted Cicely five hundred dollars, paying her in advance to make similar runs each week for five weeks. That meant whatever was in the bag was worth well over a hundred. How much was Zinnia earning from this scheme?

Although the memory of the bag in her arms roiled her stomach, Cicely knew she'd keep doing the work for as long as Zinnia wanted her. The money was too good. She'd soon have enough to pay off her debt to the Owner—maybe she could even take a week or two off from the dance hall. The last time she'd taken a vacation had been back at the Ponderosa. She could write to her mother, ask her if she could visit. The bus ticket to Orlando wouldn't cost much, and she could easily save enough to pay for a motel for a week. Or maybe her mother would invite her to stay with her. That would be nice.

Thinking such thoughts, it was easy for Cicely to forget that she was transporting what she knew was purloined human flesh.

8.

The night of that first run, Cicely slept on the cot in the bridge tower after storing the plastic bag in the fridge. Zinnia's performances at the hall had become increasingly popular and she had earned later and later time slots. That's why she couldn't be at the hospital herself at one o'clock. What happened next? Cicely didn't know. Zinnia never showed up that first night, and in the morning, Cicely caught the bus back home.

It hadn't rained in months, but it looked like it might today. Huge puffy clouds ambled together and climbed and grew dark underneath. The air felt like it was being sucked upward. Cicely huddled in the parlor with her father and listened to the Brazilian pepper trees whipping around. Dust stirred outside the front door. The edges of the tarp on the floor rattled. The room had only just lightened with morning; now it turned back to gray.

The anticipation Cicely felt outweighed anything she experienced the night before. The trip to the hospital, the nurse, the strange package—it all felt unreal. Even though she now had almost all the money for the rent, she hadn't told her father. She wanted to test him, but more than that she just didn't want to think or talk about anything except the thunderstorm she hoped would open up above them.

And then it came, the deep, phlegmy rumble over the gulf, and Cicely skipped to the front door to see if it was really happening. Beyond the threshold, it looked like nighttime. Cicely didn't know why, but it always seemed darker as the clouds approached than when the rain actually started to fall, when the black softened into a warm, bleary haze. Above the trees to the west, lightning flashed, followed a few beats later by another low roll of thunder, then more sparks of light shot out, more frequently now, and the pace of the loud cracks sped up till it all seemed like one continuous, cascading wave. The first pellets of rain that hit the roof sounded like gunshots. The plastic on the exterior snapped. Cicely felt cold drops on her face. She turned to look at her father, sitting in his chair. He was smiling. Cicely went back to her chair, sat next to him, and pulled his hand into her lap. As the rain came down in curtains and water surged in through the door and windows, neither of them said a word.

The storm crawled over the islands, then the bay, then soaked downtown and spread eastward. From what Cicely later heard, the deluge hit streets, construction sites, golf courses, farmland—washing dog shit, fertilizer, dead animals into storm drains, sewers, canals, lakes, creeks, retention ponds—flushing all the garbage that had accumulated in the months without rain down into the ground and out into the gulf. The city looked spotless, radiant.

But all that muck, that waste, that shit was food to whatever was killing life in the gulf, and before long, the piles of dead fish on the beach doubled in size. Dolphin corpses rotted in shallow waves and tiny sea turtles decomposed near the nests where they had just hatched.

It felt glorious to be alive, but the plague was worse than ever.

9.

The dance hall hosted a Cub Scout pinewood derby race on Sunday. In the name of decency, the manager told Cicely and Delanna and Hilda to wear pasties. The older boys, the ones who had attended previous races or volunteered to help on bingo night to earn a badge, barely glanced at Cicely's chest, but the younger Scouts never took their eyes off the women. Neither did the three Scoutmasters, all hall regulars, who huddled at a table near the bar chugging Mai Tais and letting the boys manage the six-grooved plastic ramp that straddled two tables up on the stage. The kids whose turn it was to race stood on chairs to release their small wooden cars, whittled and weighted, while the kids without cars clustered near the bottom of the ramp to declare the winner. Curses, threats, fists all flew. Delanna and Hilda served the boys sour pink punch while Cicely took care of the adults. Whenever the men's glasses emptied, she brought a fresh pitcher.

Cicely's eyes pulled Delanna over to the shadows draped in the corner opposite the boys. She tried to sound casual: "You never told me you hung out with Zinnia."

Delanna's forehead wrinkled. "Who told you that?"

"Zinnia."

Delanna's head slowly bobbed. "That bitch is strange." Two Scouts cheered and bumped fists. They had advanced to the next round.

"She take you to her place?"

Delanna's eyes moved from the boys to Cicely. "What are you talking about?"

Cicely looked Delanna in the face. She was cute, with soft-looking lips and brown hair that curled around behind her ears, but a blankness covered her. Cicely couldn't read her expression. "Her place," Cicely said, "Zinnia's place. Did she show you?"

"Are you messing with me?" Delanna flashed a skeptical look. "I've never hung out with that creepo."

Was she somehow in on something with Zinnia?

"Yo!" One of the Scoutmasters snapped his fingers. "More drinks!"

Cicely hesitated then shrugged. "I thought that's what she said. But you're right, a creepo. Who knows what's up with her. I figured it was bullshit."

"Waitress!"

To Delanna: "Hold on a second." Cicely refilled the Scoutmasters' six-sided pitcher.

Delanna walked back over to the boys and stood near Hilda. Cicely watched them talk under their breath. Hilda looked up and saw Cicely staring. Cicely turned and sunk back into the shadows. Hilda and Delanna spoke quietly again. Hilda laughed. A quease settled in Cicely's stomach. Her left arm, just inside the elbow, itched.

The Scoutmasters were getting drunk, and their voices grew louder as they argued about a movie. Cicely knew which film they were talking about: *No Nuts No Glory*, a regular on the bus. The driver had told her a sequel was already in the works.

Cicely watched the Scouts. They were setting up a new race, spinning their cars' plastic wheels to make sure they rolled cleanly and weighing them to make sure no one was cheating. Delanna and Hilda were no longer talking. They stood on opposite sides of the ramp, arms crossed, staring at nothing. One of the younger Scouts, severely pimpled, walked by and flipped the pink tassel on Delanna's left pasty. She slapped him. The Scoutmasters were laughing too hard to notice. As the boys began their next race, Cicely waved Delanna over again.

"What did Hilda have to say?" Cicely asked.

Delanna's head jerked back. "About what?"

"About, you know, what we were talking about."

Delanna pulled a pack of mint gum from her waistband and slowly unwrapped a stick. She took little bites as she slipped it into her mouth. "You're acting strange," she said. "You know that."

Cicely needed to change course. "How's Carlos?" she asked. Carlos was Delanna's boyfriend.

Delanna sneered. "Don't ask. We broke up. The jerk."

Fake concern now: "That's too bad. How are you doing?"

"You know, I finally offered to help him with the parasite thing. I was getting so worried it was something contagious, particularly after finding one crawling around on the toilet—"

"Oh God." Cicely had missed that twist in the story.

"So finally I ponied up the money for him to go to the doctor again and guess what, the fucker left me a week later. Said he felt guilty for relying on me for money. But has he paid me back?"

"No?"

"Of course not! He just needed an excuse! Of course it came after he got his precious fucking parasite removed. So no, don't ask me about Carlos." She said his name as if she were spitting.

One of the Scouts cheered, raised both arms over his head, and hopped in a circle. The Scoutmasters rose to their feet, clapping and swaying with booze. One of them put two fingers in his mouth and whistled.

"Does that mean we can get out of here early?" Delanna asked. "These kids are starting to get on my nerves. They're worse than the night shift losers. At least those motherfuckers tip."

10.

Two days after the rainstorm, the heat returned. The sun fell so intently on the corner where Cicely waited for the bus that her quadriceps burned inside her jeans and her nose and forehead turned pink. She hid in the slender shade of a palm trunk. By the time the bus arrived, dark stains clotted the fabric around her armpits, and the collar of her shirt was turning yellow. When she took off her flip-flops at work, the rubber straps left a curved white V on the tops of her sunburnt feet.

The manager at the dance hall allowed employees to use the industrial washing machine tucked back behind the kitchen. Each week Cicely did a small load. She brought home the clothes in a plastic garbage bag and hung them from a long piece of twine that stretched between two columns where the back porch was supposed to be. The sun hit that spot every morning and left the fabric soft and hot. It always amazed Cicely how the sun bleached her shirts whiter than any detergent. After the sun passed over them, every last stain disappeared.

When she first began taking care of her father, the intimacy of cleaning his clothes embarrassed her. Unmistakable semen stains and skid marks were common. It was disgusting enough to encounter the ooze of another body, revolting to know it belonged to her father. The first few times she did his laundry, she had to fight down the nausea that rose inside her, reminding herself it was only temporary, that he'd be back at work soon, that he too suffered when her mother abandoned them. After a year, doing the laundry simply became routine, like eating, like working—something that just happened that she never thought about, she just did, as if her hands were not a part of her.

Did he ever thank her? Clipping her shirts and his pants to the line out back, she tried to remember a time when he had, but her memory returned nothing. As she often did, she began arguing with him in her head, mouthing the words as her heart pumped with anger.

She clomped into the house, trying to make her rage obvious with each loud footfall, but he barely flinched when she came inside. Somehow he had gotten his hands on a huge stack of old issues of *National Geographic* and he was in the middle of methodically reading through each of them, even though they were so out-of-date that many of the animal species described no longer existed. He sat in his chair, surrounded by glossy covers showing pandas, rain forests, beetles, thumbing the pages and muttering. It was so hot, even inside, that he was wearing only white briefs and white socks that he pulled up to just below his knees. Small, flabby breasts flopped above his wrinkled belly.

Still fuming, Cicely tossed the gray water from the dirty bathroom bucket out onto the dirt. The clean bucket was running low. "We need more water," she said, dropping the almost-empty bucket at his feet. The little water that remained splashed.

"Now you're just wasting it," he said, not looking up from his magazine.

His voice had gotten wheezy over the last week. Was the smell from the dead fish getting to him? Cicely shut out all compassion. "Would you go get some?" An afterthought: "Please."

"Did you know polar bears have black skin underneath their fur?" He put a finger to his lips as if pondering this fact.

Cicely knocked the magazine out of his hands. It slapped onto the tarp between his feet. He dropped his head backward then gripped the armrests of his chair. He wobbled up and stuck his finger in Cicely's face. "Only because I'm in a good mood."

His breath smelled like the turkey sandwiches Cicely had brought home, and his nose throbbed slightly, as if something inside were swelling.

There was one house a couple blocks away with actual working plumbing that supplied all the Owner's half-built homes in the area. It was a ten-minute walk, tops, but Cicely's father didn't return for a half hour. He was limping. "Stepped on a fucking nail," he hissed. Cicely took the full bucket from him and helped him into his chair. His right sock was sticky with black blood.

"Papa, you need to wear your shoes." Cicely tugged gently at his sock.

"You're not helping."

He clenched his teeth as Cicely pulled off the sock. The wound was brown and deep, but at least the nail hadn't gotten stuck. She dipped one of his clean shirts in the fresh water and scrubbed gently around the hole. Her father gasped. "I know, I know," she said, "but I've got to." She poured more clean water. It ran down the bottom of his foot, a pale pink, and splattered on the cover of the *National Geographic* she had knocked out of his hands. When the wound was as clean as it would get, Cicely spun the shirt into a long, thick roll and tied it loosely around his foot, then set the injured appendage down on the tarp. "We'll have to watch for infection," she said. "Tell me if it starts looking black."

All he said was, "We'll need more water." He closed his eyes. From where Cicely crouched, she could see up into his bushy nostrils.

Still no thank you, never a thank you. Cicely grumbled to herself as she carried the empty bucket down the street to the house with the plumbing. Some of the homes she passed had doors and windows, some even had new-looking metal roofs and tall fences and verdant lawns, but even those homes, still occupied, still maintained, looked lifeless. Tightly shut blinds blocked any view inside, but Cicely could see the glow of lamps and chandeliers playing on the white slats. At one house, a crew of sunburnt men with bandannas tied over their mouths mowed and clipped and edged. At another, a man in paint-splattered white jeans climbed a ladder to nail in a new gutter. Even after years of living just steps away, Cicely still had no idea who lived in these homes. She saw cars coming and going, but never saw kids playing in the street, never heard backyard parties. What did they think of Cicely and her kind? If they thought of them at all. But they must see the severed drainpipes, the dirty crowds at the bus stop, the poor who gathered for free food from St. Mark's. The city's rich had been remote to Cicely her entire life, but since the crash, except for at the dance hall, the wealthy had grown invisible. How those with homes spent their weekends, where their kids went to school, what they ate for dinner—it was like their lives were hidden behind a curtain that Cicely didn't have the energy to tug at.

Two old women formed a line at the working sink in the house ten lots down while a third filled up a huge clear jug. Cicely recognized the women but didn't say hi. She just nodded politely when they turned to look at her and then she looked down at her feet. She pitied their muumuus and jelly sandals and wobbly knees and scorched hair, but these women also made her feel embarrassed, because she knew, and they knew, and she knew they knew, that her life bore a stronger resemblance to theirs than any twenty-five-year-old would want to admit. She didn't see her future in their bent spines and worked-down shoulders—she saw her own life.

The woman at the front of the line finished filling her enormous jug. How would she get it home? She picked it up, stumbled a few feet, then slammed it back on the ground, then repeated herself. It would take her an hour to go a block. As the next woman in line stepped up to the faucet, Cicely set down her bucket and went to help the first woman. "Where are you going?" she asked, placing her hand on the old woman's wrist. Cicely always touched old people delicately, as if even the gentlest physical contact might break them.

Huffing, with her hands on her hips, the old woman drew

back and squinted at Cicely. She scratched at a triangle of moles on the left side of her neck. "Who are you?" The words sounded tired, as if this interaction were just another chore.

"Can I help you?"

"I've been carrying this thing back and forth for three years. One more trip isn't going to kill me." She wrapped her hands around the jug's handle and lugged it a few more steps. When the jug hit the ground again, it made a sloshing, sucking sound. As Cicely watched her lug her water home, step by exhausted step, another old woman arrived and took Cicely's place in line.

11.

Cicely screamed when she saw the snake rustling beneath the tarp. Living without doors and windows, she had become accustomed to frogs, lizards, squirrels, and raccoons scampering through the house, but she could never get used to snakes.

This one was vermilion, with rings of black and white. Its head poked out from underneath the corner of the tarp nearest the stairs; its slender body scratched at the blue plastic. Cicely leapt onto her chair. Her father was out front pissing. "Papa!" she shouted, her toes wiggling in fear as she bounced up and down on the seat cushion. "Papa!" The snake rolled out from underneath the tarp, heading in the direction of the stairs. "Papa!"

When her father entered, he was still zipping himself up. When he saw her mad pointing and then saw the snake lying there on the concrete between the tarp and the stairs, he smirked. "If red touches yellow, it can kill a fellow," he said, stepping carefully around the tarp and toward the bathroom. He tiptoed back with a bucket. "If red touches black...." He inched toward the snake and lowered the lip of the bucket. "It is a friend of Jack." With one quick dip, her father scooped the snake's head into the bucket then flipped its tail up and in. He held it out for Cicely to see: "It's harmless."

"That may be," Cicely said, waving him off. "Doesn't mean I want him in my living room." She hopped back onto the floor.

Her father kept staring into the bucket. "I forget what these are called," he said, "but we used to see them in the dunes every now and then when I was a kid. Those spots were wild back then. Some kids and I used to set up targets and shoot BB guns out there and sometimes we'd try to wing critters, too."

Cicely rubbed her hands together. "Shoot all the snakes you want."

"I shot a friend of mine once." He chuckled.

"What?"

"On accident, on accident." He shook the bucket. Cicely could hear the snake's scales rubbing against the plastic. "And besides, it was a BB. My friend had gone into the pines back behind the dunes while I was shooting at this little lizard, and the lizard was sitting on this ridge, and so when I missed, the BBs went whizzing off behind the dune." He blew softly on the snake. "The kid for some dumb reason came back from the trees by a different route, so he ended up right on the other side of this lizard, but I couldn't see over the ridge. Yeah, I winged him."

Cicely had to laugh. "Where'd you hit him?"

Her father scratched at the right side of his neck. "Around here. He said it didn't really hurt, but he was still pissed." He shrugged. "It was a strange sight—this little gold pellet dug into someone's skin. We helped him pop it out. There was a little blood, I guess."

"And what about the lizard?" Steeling herself, she leaned over the bucket and looked down. The snake lay hunkered down in about an inch of water, its head gently shifting left and right, its dark eyes unreadable. Black scales formed a tiny little cap on top of its skull; its snout grew wide and flat at the tip. It seemed neither angry nor afraid.

"The what?" her father asked. He rattled the bucket and the snake's head banged into the plastic walls.

"The lizard, the lizard," Cicely said. "The one you were shooting at."

"Oh, oh, that." He took two steps toward the front door. "By the time we got the BB out of the kid, it was long gone." He walked out into the dusty lot, and tossed the snake far into a tangle of Jamaica caper trees. It landed with a soft thud.

Cicely leaned against the front of the home and watched as the snake oscillated into deeper foliage. The relief it must have felt, if it felt, the escape from the terror of a foreign home, the confusion, too. People used to have doors and windows, it must have remembered. At least it didn't dine on fish, so it remained untouched by one calamity.

Cicely's father pulled down his pants and resumed urinating.

12.

"Placentas?"

Zinnia offered to buy Cicely lunch to celebrate week two of their arrangement. They sat across from each other at a long wooden table set on a bayside dock. A thick, clear plastic curtain had been pulled down around the dock to keep out the rotting fish smell, but the plastic also blocked whatever breeze there was, and sitting inside it felt like being basted in a wet oven. Cicely didn't want to know where the place was buying its seafood from these days.

"Placentas."

The word itself sounded strange. What did a placenta look like? Cicely had no way to connect those syllables to the contents of the bag she hauled away from the hospital. How many placentas were in that bag? How had the nurse gotten them away from the delivery rooms? Who was buying them?

"Is that a problem?" Zinnia looked at Cicely as if she knew it wasn't. She slowly poured blond beer into a plastic cup; the foam crept over the rim. Zinnia drained the bottle of its last sip then chucked the glass into a garbage pail a few feet away. Zinnia shook salt onto her palm and licked it before taking a big swig from the cup. She sighed with pleasure.

Something that grows inside you. Something you aren't born with. Something that takes shape well after you're grown. Cicely had gotten used to the idea that her body was hers, that it wouldn't change till she began to die. But pregnancy, this idea that a body could grow again in ways she had never known and could never anticipate: foreign.

Right before Cicely dropped out of high school, her best friend Cris—"Spelled with a 'C'," she reminded everyone, always—got knocked up by a skater. Cicely was there when she found out. Cris had dragged her to the drugstore and forced her to buy the test. She knew Cicely's mom had split, knew her dad was falling apart, figured there was nobody to get mad if Cicely got spotted instead of her. They took the bus way south, far away from anywhere anyone from school might go, and Cris leaned against the fungal-smelling dumpster out back while Cicely went inside.

Cicely waved to the clerk in the red polo at the front desk. His eyes looked dead. Cicely puttered down the aisle with chips and pretzels, pretending to look at ingredients, then slowly made her way back to the section marked Family Planning. Condoms—too late for that. She smiled and brushed past the shiny boxes and leaned down to snag the cheapest store-brand pregnancy test. When she stood up, a woman in a white lab coat behind the pharmacy counter was staring right at her. A moment of panic. Did she know her? But the instant passed, and the woman's gaze drifted back to her clipboard. Cicely suddenly saw herself through this woman's eyes: fifteen, wearing an olive green pleated skirt that hung to her knees and stocky black boots with pink laces, backpack slung over one shoulder, white men's shirt unbuttoned so low you could see her bra, ballpoint pen scribbles up and down the inside of each forearm, song lyrics and little filled-in stars, three studs in her left ear, one in her right, standing in this aisle, planning her family, but not really, just trying to help a friend. But this woman didn't know that, couldn't see that. Would Cris walk into this store for her? Would anyone?

Cicely paid with Cris's money and walked out, back to the dumpster. The parking lot bordered a miniature golf course and a stream of Buddy Holly and Chuck Berry hits wafted down from loudspeakers strung up on poles around the course. Cris didn't want to wait, so she ducked between the dumpster and the beige wall of the store and yanked down her jeans. Cicely turned her head, but she could still hear the splatter and smell the yellow animal smell. When Cris was done, she handed the plastic stick to Cicely while she pulled up her pants. The test felt so light. Cris paced. Three minutes dragged by. "What does two bars mean?" Cicely asked. Cris started crying.

When Cicely dropped out, she and Cris lost touch. That was what, ten years ago? It didn't seem possible. At various jobs since, women had gotten pregnant and been forced to quit—no one Cicely ever felt close to. Motherhood was like an affliction, something that happened to you and took you away. For the other servers at the dance hall, the idea was abominable. For Cicely, being dragged away from this life sounded like a blessing.

"Who buys them?" Cicely rubbed the sticky rim of her beer bottle with her thumb.

Zinnia shook her head and raised her cup. "Let's just enjoy this for now."

More questions pressed in on Cicely. Not just who bought the placentas, but what they used them for. What good were they after they were spit out? But at this moment, forgetting felt all right.

"Do you write your own songs?" Cicely asked.

"I mix and match," Zinnia said. "Maybe half the stuff you've heard is original." She looked out through the wall of plastic. The shore around the dock was mostly one long concrete wall, so there was nowhere for the dead fish to wash up. Still, some corpses bobbed in the waves a few dozen feet out. The small fishing boats, which you would normally see swimming in and out of the bay, were all tied to rusty cleats screwed into the seawall.

Cicely's beer tasted sour. "I can't even begin to understand how you write a song. How someone writes a song, I mean."

Zinnia put both hands on the table, palms down. "It's pretty formulaic. A friend told me about a story she read on the internet about a computer that analyzed melodies and how they plugged in all these songs, stuff from way back all the way up to last year. And that really there are three, maybe four melodies out there. Everything else is just tiny variations."

"I don't even listen to music much. Just whatever's in the movies." Cicely knew she sounded ignorant.

"That's most people, though. Most people don't have time for much more than that. And think about the music in those movies. All those songs sound exactly the same." Zinnia leaned back and folded her hands together. "It's like once they figured out the quickest route to jamming something into your brain, they forgot everything else."

"That's what people want, I guess."

Zinnia slapped the table with her hands. The pitch of her voice rose. "Fucking A, they do. But someone still has to be out there giving it to them."

Cicely's parents owned a radio when she was growing up, but they never played music. For years, Cicely thought radios were only good for picking up football. But at some point, Cicely's mother had found an old Discman at Goodwill and started checking out CDs from the library. The two of them would share the headphones back and forth on the bus on the way to the beach, on Sundays. Her mom loved singer-songwriter stuff from the Seventies. Cicely knew the music was lame but didn't complain. She just loved to hear the voices, particularly those in the background, the second or third layers that you never paid attention to at first. But when you listened to the same song over and over, those were the ones that started to stand out, the singer's lonely friends, singing along even though they knew no one would ever hear them. Cicely remembered the Christmas when a ton of kids at school first got mp3 players. She asked her parents for one too, but they couldn't afford it. Instead, Cicely's mom gave her the Discman to keep for herself, and Cicely began checking out her own CDs from the library. Given total freedom, she still always returned to those discs her mom loved, even after her mother left.

"But you've got fans."

"Ha. Twenty guys, losers all."

The bartender called out to Zinnia to come pick up their food. She grabbed the red plastic baskets lined with wax paper and piled with fried fish, while Cicely pulled out handfuls of brown napkins and ordered more beer. The food smelled divine—like grassy oil and golden salt. Grease stained the wax paper. When Cicely broke a piece of fish in two, steam poured out of its white meat. She blew on it. What color was a placenta? Red, she figured. Like most everything else inside us. But wait. Was that even true?

Zinnia broke into her thoughts: "Truth is, those guys have been listening to me for years. But when was the last time I saw someone new out there? It kills me to picture myself ten years from now, playing wherever, and looking out into the audience and seeing the same faces."

Cicely laughed, almost spitting fish. "But even that's something. You've got to be happy with what you've got."

"Pffft." Zinnia wagged a French fry at her. "Fuck that. You think I like driving placentas around?" The bartender, packing the cooler with ice, looked over. Realizing she was speaking too loudly, Zinnia began talking more quietly. "I'm trying to get out of here."

"Oh come on, it's the same everywhere." Cicely felt the rush of actual conversation. She and Zinnia were sitting together—drinking, eating, talking. Her legs rubbed together; her thighs warmed and tingled. She mashed a spoonful of cole slaw between her teeth and spoke before swallowing: "Maybe there aren't dead fish everywhere, but there's something horrible everywhere, I guarantee you."

"I can't think like that." Zinnia was chewing on a fry. "I just can't."

Maybe Cicely was wrong. What was Orlando like? Had her mother chosen that place? Or was it just another place to get stuck? That morning, the morning Cicely woke up and found her father bawling in the kitchen, crying because he didn't know how to use the coffee pot and it had spilled over, tossing wet grounds all over the floor, the morning her mother left, did her mother leave the house knowing exactly where she was going? Did she have a plan? At first, Cicely thought her mother must have, that she knew exactly where she was headed, but as Cicely got older, she changed her mind. Her mother's flight must have been chaotic. She must have been scared. Cicely pictured her out in the street in front of their house, taking one last look back, maybe even taking a step back toward the front door, the cicadas roaring in her ears, before she turned around.

"Have you ever been to Orlando?"

"That doesn't count." Zinnia waved a hand, as if Cicely were just trying to prove a point.

"No, really. My mom lives there. I've never been."

Zinnia wiped her lips. "Total shithole."

The beer was beginning to make everything a little wobbly. Out in the bay, a yacht was powering by, headed for the gulf. Its engine roared. A pelican circled above the wake, its shadow a flickering gray cloud rising and falling in the waves that angled away from the boat. The bird dove and splashed into the water. Spray from its flapping wings clouded outward as it climbed back into the burning sky.

Cicely's knees had come together. The seams in her denim kissed. She needed to pee, but she didn't want to interrupt the conversation. She squeezed her pelvic floor muscles and her crotch shook. Warm, juicy flakes of fish broke apart in her mouth. Her lips tasted like seawater. It was hot inside the plastic walls, and Cicely felt moisture gathering around the edge of her hair. She had slipped her sandals off and was rubbing the warm grooves of the dock with her toes.

Zinnia was telling some story about the last time she visited Orlando, part of some tour, but Cicely wasn't listening. She was watching Zinnia's mouth move, trying to count the crinkles in her pale lips, bending in to see if she could catch a glimpse of a molar or two, wondering why she didn't lick away that small bit of potato from the left corner of her mouth, trying to figure out what she would have eaten that would have made the top of her tongue so red.

It took Cicely a few moments to realize Zinnia had stopped talking. All she could do was laugh: "I didn't hear a word of that." Zinnia's lips met in a warm smile. Cicely pushed away her empty basket and guzzled more beer. She liked being with someone who wouldn't snap at her when she did something stupid or weird. At that moment, she didn't care about her parents, the man with the box cutter, the fact that she needed to be at work in a few hours. She ordered another round and told Zinnia she'd cover it. Zinnia's smile never broke.

Outside, the pelican that had been circling began to wobble. It beat its shaky wings, trying to rise, and it did, for a moment, before plunging down again, this time dead. It smacked into the shimmering waters of the bay with an ugly plop.

13.

The ten fifties felt strange in her fingers. She had never noticed money's texture—its soft, woven grids. She liked Grant's face, the bulbous mole or whatever it was that sprouted from his right cheek, his odd tie, looped and folded on one side and a crisp point on the other. Up close, his suit looked like it was made of tiny bricks. At first, Cicely thought the patterns that ran along the top and bottom looked like spiderwebs, but when she looked more closely, the dense scratches just grew denser, more complex than any web something living could invent. Cicely rubbed her middle finger and thumb together. A trace of ink or dirt, something black, had come off, had stamped the tiny waves of her fingerprints. Cicely had a habit of picking off the edges of her fingernails when they grew too long, and all her nails had been clawed down close to the skin, with small yellow and brown dots of dirt trapped underneath. At least she kept her cuticles neat—those were pushed far back, up the nail, behind the broad elliptic leaf of white.

Cicely counted the bills for the fourth time and put them back in the envelope along with the cash she had saved from work and she tucked the package back into the insulation. It was Tuesday—Father Bill's day—and she needed to get dressed. She was still wearing just her bra and panties; it made the heat bearable. As she slipped on her dress, she reveled in small sensations. The dress hugged her tightly around the waist and the folds below flitted against her calves and knees. Zipping herself up tightened her chest. She didn't have a mirror upstairs, but she knew she looked beautiful.

Downstairs, her father was looping together his tie. Cicely gave it a final tug and spread his collar down over it. Her father's silences had different flavors—over the years Cicely had learned to distinguish them with just a glance. Today, he was bent over, his bones sagging, and the ring of fat that circled his belly hung out just a little more than usual. He'd be grouchy. But Cicely, feeling light with the memory of the money, her secret in the insulation, and the rustle of the dress around her, didn't care. Normally when he was grumpy she'd tiptoe around him, trying not to disturb him. This morning, she just asked what she wanted to ask: "Did you ever visit the VFW? The rent is due day after tomorrow."

"Don't act like your mother." He spit the words. "She used to do that. Don't act like that."

Cicely wanted to laugh. He thought he could hurt her, but he had no clue what she had hidden upstairs. What if she just took her money and left? Shacked up with Zinnia and started driving more routes? What would he do then? Die, probably. But not even that thought could smother Cicely's good humor. She tried to sound concerned: "But what are we going to do, Papa?"

Her tone was a touch too light. She could see that he knew she was making fun of him. He looked away from her, toward the dust and broken shells out front. "She'd stand there looking right at the lawn, overgrown and all crazy, and ask me if I had cut it yet," he said. "She could see damn well I hadn't cut it."

Her mother had done the same with Cicely. "Did you clean up your room?" her mother would ask, as if she were blind to the Legos and G.I. Joes scattered about. That was what being a grownup meant, Cicely remembered thinking: not saying what you mean.

"I remember that too, Papa."

Her father rocked back and forth. He squeezed his mouth with his left hand. Air shot out of his nostrils. "It's funny how you can feel nostalgic even for the bad stuff."

It was difficult to imagine ever, in the future, looking back fondly on these times, but Cicely knew it was possible. Things could always get worse.

As tender as she felt for him at that moment, she didn't want to give up the charade of not having money for the rent. She touched him lightly on the arm, bringing his attention back to her. "The man with the box cutter is coming Thursday, and we don't have enough."

Beneath her touch, he turned cold. "Can't you just fuck some guys at work," he said. "That should be worth, what, ten, fifteen bucks?"

It felt like her chest caved in. She stepped back and put a hand on the kitchen counter to steady herself. Words whipped inside her, but all she came out with was: "God damn you, God damn you." She was getting louder. "God damn you." She stepped forward and grabbed his tie, pulling it down so that he bent forward, then she shoved him in the chest with both hands. He accepted the abuse. "You have no idea!" Her heart thundered. She went close to him, grabbed his collar with both hands. His arms hung by his sides—he made no effort to stop her or strike back. She pulled his face close to hers. She wanted to tell him she hated him, that he would die without her, that it was only her, her shitty job, that kept him alive, that whatever pitiful life he led was all due to her, that he was nothing but a brute, a hunk of meat she was chained to, that without her he'd be drinking rainwater from a storm sewer, that he'd probably be out on the beach eating the dead fish right now, that he was no father, never was a father, that if men thought they had created this world, that they were so proud of that, to just look the fuck around some time and see what all that had come to. None of that made its way out. She sputtered: "Why are you like this?"

She pushed him again then turned for the door and slipped outside. Although she was starving, she couldn't bear the thought of listening to Father Bill drone on this morning. She stomped along the path out to the beach, not bothering to push branches away from her face, letting them scratch her. Tears whooshed out of her now, but she didn't slow down.

Ducking under the bridge, she walked into a sudden wall of rotten fish odor. The current here tugged at the bodies that had collected between the stones that lay in the shade of the bridge. The liches oozed. The scene nauseated Cicely and her stomach flopped. Her mouth filled with saliva as she rushed through the shadows.

The smell on the other side of the bridge was still terrible, but at least the breeze didn't allow it to settle. When she made it to the mangroves, she collapsed into the damp sand, sobbing. Her dress grew wet and dirty, but she didn't care. She rolled onto her side.

Half-buried a few feet in front of her lay a silver and gold condom wrapper. May cause allergic reaction, Cicely read. She rolled onto her back. The mangrove branches criss-crossed tightly above her, blocking out most of the sky, but she could still spy low clouds blowing through the blue. Her mane, which she had patiently combed, now twisted around her, clogged with sand. All feeling slowly drained out of her. Her limbs felt lifeless and heavy. Closing her eyes was an act of extreme peace.

Startled, she jerked upright. How long had she been out? It was still daytime, but the angle of light had shifted. Her face felt crusty with dried snot; her insides were empty. But she had slept well, and the world around her was in focus. Every leaf shivered in its place; every stone bore a message.

Cicely sniffled and laughed then stood up and brushed the sand off her dress. It was still damp, and stained in spots, but cleaning it wouldn't be impossible. Slipping off her soft flats, she felt her toes sink into the wet sand. Sleeping on the ground had chilled her—feeling cold felt good. She stepped back onto the path, turning toward the beach rather than home. The route slipped through low dunes shot through with twisty roots. Cicely groaned in pain when she stepped on a prickly burr and hopped up and down on one foot while she dislodged it from the thick crust of her heel. She put her sandals back on till the path widened out onto the beach itself.

Someone—the county? the state?—had dispatched men in hazmat suits to dispose of the dead fish. A team scurried from one pile of fish to another, spearing the corpses with long metal sticks and placing them in reinforced plastic bags. Maybe she shouldn't be out here. But the air smelled the same as it had for the last week, for days she had been breathing it, so what good was protecting herself now?

She walked to the north, her eyes down so she could dodge desiccated fish parts. The humidity felt like a prison. She looked up the beach. A seagull was plucking out the eye of a dead fish. Stupid bird. It would die, too. Cicely ran a few steps, waving her arms till the gull relented and flew away, squawking at her. On those Sundays when she used to come to the beach with her mother, she loved to chase birds. She'd scatter potato chips to draw a crowd then turn on them, running right at them and diving to grasp at their brittle legs. Her mother told her she shouldn't bother innocent creatures, but she still laughed when Cicely lunged and the birds scattered.

The hazmat team was dragging their full bags back to their truck. The area they had covered was clear, but it was just a small part of the beach. To finish the job would take weeks. And that was assuming nothing more would wash up.

Cicely thought of her mother's letter, the one about the beach. She dropped to her hands and knees, looking for the fragile tunnels that the crabs dug. She found one and scooped out the sand around it, but no crab emerged. She tried a few more, but there was no life there, either. Sitting back on her legs, she stared out at a yacht bobbing in the gulf. A woman in a coral-colored bikini and some kind of mask—yes, it was a gas mask—lay sunbathing on the yacht's wooden deck, while a sunburned man swam in circles around the boat. He, too, wore a mask.

14.

Dwayne, one of the bartenders at the hall, called her over the next night. On the bar top lay another envelope, just like the other two from her mother, except this one carried a mug-sized ring of moisture.

"Using this as a coaster?" Cicely asked. As she reached for the envelope, Dwayne leaned in and put his hand over hers. She yanked her arm back. Dwayne was one of the bartenders who sold pills from under the counter. His eyes looked faded. He licked his lips, wetting the tips of his overgrown mustache.

"Who's the lucky guy?" he asked.

"None of your business."

Dwayne's muscles rolled as he stood up straight. His yellow T-shirt clutched his chest and shoulders. "Just strange to be getting so much mail." He nodded his head toward Zinnia, who was wrapping up her set. "This wouldn't have anything to do with your dalliance with, uh, you know who. Would it?"

Worried he might see her face turn red, Cicely turned away.

Dwayne chuckled. "Your secret's safe with me."

Bathed in red light, Zinnia sang about how falling in love felt like being dismembered.

Dwayne cocked his head back and looked down at Cicely. "I would just advise that you think hard about branching out into"—he put his hands down on the scratched bartop—"new markets."

He didn't know anything. He probably just heard gossip from Delanna and Hilda, was worried about his side business. Cicely faked a laugh and walked away, tucking the letter in her pocket. The first letter mystified her, the second excited her, this one left her indifferent. She'd been stewing about the fight with her father. She hadn't seen him since she had shoved him. He hadn't come home last night. It had happened before—he'd be arrested, spend a night or two in jail for vagrancy—but they'd never fought like that. It never got physical. Cicely didn't regret pushing him, truly, but she didn't like having done it either. Even if he was pissed, she knew he'd come back. He always did. In the past, when she wished he wouldn't come back, she stopped herself from thinking that way. Now she made no such effort.

The hall was packed, but the evening dragged. Zinnia left the keys to the van with Cicely before starting the second half of her set and promised to drive Cicely home in the morning. She kissed her on the cheek and wished her good luck. Cicely changed into her jeans and tank top and walked to the van. The heat, normally suffocating, now felt comforting, like rolling a blanket over you when you're still fully dressed and too sleepy to care. Cicely turned the key and the van shook to life. Traffic was almost nonexistent on the ride over to the hospital, but Cicely passed two cop cars, both idling on side streets.

She got to Delphine and Azalea way too early—around twelve forty—so she circled and circled and circled the block. Was that more or less conspicuous than just parking? She'd have to ask Zinnia. The van's radio worked, and Cicely rotated the dial till she found old jazz. She didn't like jazz, but anything was preferable to silence, or to the movie anthems that dominated the other stations. Stately cymbal taps punctuated her circling; the bass moaned. The E in the emergency room sign had still not been fixed; now the final O was blinking, too. An ambulance screamed up and then left. A helicopter swished away from one of the rooftops.

At exactly twelve fifty-eight Cicely parked the van, this time on the opposite side of the footbridge, farther away from the ER. She remembered the nurses, the flat tire, the guy using the cell phone. No way she was exposing herself like that again. And she had remembered not to bother about the coat. Her ribbed white tank top squeezed her breasts, her arms grew sticky in the heat, and her hair curled.

Squeak, squeak. The sneaker sound broke into Cicely's pacing. Cicely waved up at the pink-headed nurse, mouthing, "Hey." The nurse mouthed back then tossed the bag—same color, same size. As it fell, Cicely realized she had misjudged her spot. She lunged to her right to catch it, but the bag hit the pavement with a splotch. Christ. What had she done? Were placentas delicate? Zinnia had not prepared her for missing the bag, for dropping it. After all, what could be simpler than catching a bag someone dropped. She looked at the green bag on the ground and then glanced up at the footbridge, but the nurse was gone. If the placentas were ruined it wasn't the nurse's fault; it was Cicely's.

She took two steps toward the bag and bent down. The package seemed so small lying there, just outside a ring of streetlight that beamed down on the scene. Afraid to just grab it, Cicely gripped a corner and pulled it toward her. It still seemed solid; nothing seemed to have splattered inside. But could she really tell? She lifted it carefully and tried to figure out how many placentas there might be inside. But she couldn't differentiate shapes. It all seemed like a gelatinous whole, a mix of soft muscle and sinew. Was she transporting five placentas? Twenty? And how much were they worth, in the end? An awful lot to someone, whomever Zinnia sold them to. Cicely shuffled over to the van, holding the bag between her forearms, extended straight out like a forklift. She had been careless before; now her actions were impeccable. Into the cooler. Under the ice. And there was Cicely, back in the driver's seat, igniting the engine. The clock on the dash said one ten. It took thirty minutes to get to the bridge tower.

Placentas tucked safely in fridge, Cicely lay on Zinnia's cot. She wanted to be awake when Zinnia returned, so she chewed on a lime wedge. The acid bit into her gums.

Cicely hadn't just lain down and thought in over a year.

Exhaustion always killed her worries. She never tossed and turned, never wandered the house or took walks to wear herself out. Just getting through the day was victory. Not tonight, though. When was the last time she thought about the day after tomorrow? Or the week after next? A torrent of fantasies overtook her. She lived in a downtown condo and dressed for work in a business suit. She parked her own car in a garage beneath the building. She lived alone but threw parties. She met a man who knew how to dice an onion. She took trips to Mexico. She knew people who invited her on boats. She got pregnant on purpose. She bought coffee for female friends. She danced at weddings. She slept in on the weekends in a bed topped with a puffy comforter. She set the air-conditioner to the temperature she liked. She had running water.

The green canvas cot was raw and scratchy on the back of her neck. She turned and faced the gray wall, decorated here and there with Sharpie genitals. As ugly, as basic, as it was, she loved this space. A helicopter buzzed by, its high beam lighting up the inside of the tower for a moment. Below, delicate waves nuzzled the concrete pillars that held up the bridge. From far off, in the fishing village, the plaintive whine of a steel guitar floated over. It sounded live, and Cicely could just make out other noises, little bursts of cheers, like someone was hosting a party.

The black of the night turned into a deeper black then an even deeper black. As hard as she tried to fight it, Cicely fell asleep.

When Zinnia shook her awake, morning was already near. The first words out of Cicely's mouth were, "Who do you sell them to?"

Zinnia sat down on the cot. Her shadow leaned over Cicely. Her face seemed to be asking: you really want to know?

Cicely nodded.

Zinnia's weight on the cot made Cicely roll closer. The fabric stretched and groaned. "A doula," Zinnia said, then stood up. "She sells them to mothers who are hooked on them." The lights from the condos on the barrier island twinkled. "They eat them."

15.

By the time she made it back home, the yellow truck that belonged to the man with the box cutter was idling out front. She felt cocky knowing the money was upstairs in the wall. If the man with the box cutter had been forced to wait for an hour, so be it. She walked behind the grumbling truck, its wheels as tall as her, and stepped into the house. There he was, sitting in her chair, fiddling with a cell phone. The first thing she noticed was the baby blue box cutter, tucked inside his belt on the right side. Its long, curving body was a menace; Cicely could just see the silver tip of the blade inside the broad slit in the tool's end. The man's jeans were tight and rode high—they ended above his ankles—and he wore heavy tan work boots whose shafts he had sawed off. The boots barely covered the bump of his heel. The man's T-shirt was tight, too, with a short straight cut down from the front of the collar to give it some give. When he looked up as Cicely walked in, blond corn rows flailed around his head and the beads at the tips click-clacked. A broad red bandanna crept low on his forehead. His expression broadcast annoyance.

"Once a month," he said. "You have to be here, on time, once a month."

"You'll get your money," she said. The tarp crinkled beneath her sandals.

He balanced his phone on his knee. He had been watching a movie. Cicely recognized the paused image from the bus, but couldn't remember the name of the film. "I know," he said. The fingers of his right hand grazed the handle of the box cutter.

"There's no need for that. It's upstairs." When Cicely reached the foot of the staircase, he went back to his phone. This guy didn't rule her life, he wasn't in charge anymore than she was, but she hated him anyway. When her back went crooked with the weight of the water bucket, when a customer at the hall eyed her butt a little too long, when a fight broke out on the bus, it was this guy's face she saw. She was happy she wasted his time, happy she was going to fling money in his face.

Before heading to the slit in the insulation, she looked back down the stairs to make sure he was still sitting there watching the movie. She didn't want anyone to know her hiding spot. His gaze stayed stuck to the screen.

She slipped around the corner, past her mattress and toward the rear of the home. The hole in the wall was right next to a square that had been cut out for a window. From the second story, Cicely could see over the trees just a bit. The bay sparkled in the distance. A biplane slowly cruised back and forth above the downtown skyline, dragging a long banner with immense text: Father Bill says give and you shall be given to. Cicely smirked as she reached into the wall and parted the soft lining where lay her envelope.

Except it wasn't there.

Heat rose in Cicely's body. Her hand clutched up, down, left, right. Nothing. She pulled on the insulation till it puffed out of the hole. She pried open the slit, tore the insulation apart. God, it wasn't there. Cicely's face felt feverish. Her stomach shook. Her father. She knew right away it had been her father. He had known about this place all along. That's why he disappeared. He hadn't been arrested. Her wrists twitched. She couldn't believe it—she suddenly needed to shit. Right now. Her insides had gone liquid. She leaned over and squeezed every muscle she could. But it helped for only a moment. She tripped down the hall to the upstairs bathroom. The water didn't work, but it was either the toilet or her pants. As soon as she sat down her guts loosened. Relief. But her feet wouldn't stay still. Her heels tap-tap-tapped on the raw, untiled floor.

"Fee fi fo fum," the man downstairs bellowed. His boots made the stairs creak.

Cicely quickly wiped herself with stolen brown napkins she kept by the toilet and pulled up her jeans. She was just exiting the bathroom when the man appeared at the top of the stairs. She raised her hands, palms toward him. "Listen, I swear I had the money. I swear I have the money. I mean, not here, but I have it." Her breath was slowing. She pointed to the hole in the wall. "Someone stole it."

His eyes looked so quiet. He walked right toward her.

"I swear, I swear." She backed up into the bathroom.

He followed her, his nose wrinkling at the smell from the toilet. With a quick jab, he grabbed her by the upper arm and pulled her out into the hallway. She stumbled as he pushed her from behind, toward her hiding place.

"I swear. It was here yesterday." She turned to face him and stepped back against the wall. "It's gone, it's gone."

The box cutter was suddenly in his hand, its blade beginning to creep out. He stepped right up to her. His breath smelled like a dog's. His left hand gripped her face, covering her mouth. The back of her skull banged into the wall. The box cutter nipped her arm. Blood slipped out. He put the blade to her cheek. So close, she could tell it wasn't even sharp, was in fact rusty. The buzz from the plane still reverberated in the room. Cicely closed her eyes and tensed her whole body.

When he loosened his grip, she collapsed. The floor rushed at her. His boots filled her vision. They moved to the left. She looked up. He reached into the hole in the wall, cutting up the insulation with his blade.

Him, irritated: "Who did it?"

Without thinking, it came out: "My dad, my dad."

Tsk-tsk. "Her own father," he whispered.

This man felt sorry for her. She kept discovering new lows. She wailed.

He grabbed her arm again and yanked her to her feet. "No time for that." He pushed her toward the stairs, gently this time. "Let's go." He smiled. For the first time, she noticed he wore gold stars on his four front teeth.

16.

Cicely shielded her eyes from the glare in the windows of the Owner's downtown office building as the truck pulled into the adjacent garage.

The man with the box cutter nudged her from behind, toward the elevator. Inside, he punched the button for floor twenty-nine. Floor thirty required a key.

The elevator opened to a chilly lobby. Posters advertising the virtues of Persistence, Vision, and Achievement and adorned with photos of the Grand Canyon, the Colosseum, and the Taj Mahal hung on the walls. Lifeless keyboard pop trickled out from a hidden speaker. A woman in a gray business suit sat behind the lobby's tall, glass-topped desk, empty except for a phone, a keyboard, a mouse, and an enormous flat computer screen. The man with the box cutter pointed to a chair. Cicely slumped. Whatever anger she felt, whatever resistance she might have offered, had all drained away. The secretary eyed her over gray rectangular glasses then turned her attention to the man with the box cutter. They whispered to each other and the woman nodded, clicking something on her computer.

"We wait," the man said, settling into the chair to Cicely's left. The chairs were egg-shaped, with blue fabric softer than anything Cicely had sat on for a very long time. Even through her sandals, Cicely could tell that the hard white floor was frigid. The man turned his phone back on and resumed watching his movie. As he watched, he slurped on a tamarind candy, and when he laughed, brown spit hit the screen. Cicely suddenly recalled the name of the movie: *Gonad Gone Mad*. The volume was just loud enough that she couldn't ignore the laugh track.

The elevator dinged. Brown package. Ding again. Brown package needing signature. How long had she been waiting? Fifteen minutes? It seemed like hours. What did the Owner have in store for her? Fear rattled inside her, but Cicely guessed she wasn't in immediate jeopardy. If something bad was going to happen, it wouldn't happen here, where he worked, where there was all this nice furniture. But still, those stories Delanna had told her. When she first heard them they sounded farfetched—why throw someone who owes you money off a bridge?—but she couldn't entirely discount them, either. She touched the cut on her arm. It hadn't quite healed, but the blood had dried into a maroon crust. It flaked away beneath her fingers. The man hadn't cut her cheek, but she could tell he had scratched her. It itched. What were these men capable of?

She stood. The man looked up from his phone. His eyes said, Sit down.

"Stretching my legs."

He returned to his screen.

Her sandals flapped against the floor as she paced the perimeter of the lobby. Persistence. Vision. Achievement. Persistence. Vision. Achievement. Persistence—I've got that, Cicely thought. Many women would have given up a long time ago. Many, in fact, had. Women Cicely knew had killed themselves, gone crazy, started sleeping on the streets. Vision—no. Fantasies, yes, hopes, yes, vision, no. Achievement—no. Unless you counted survival. The Achievement poster was the one with the image of the Colosseum on it. How strange. Was building a place for people to murder one another really such an achievement? The secretary eyed Cicely as she circled the room.

After an hour or so, the door to the Owner's office swung open and the man with the box cutter stood up and nodded to her: "Go on." The tamarind candy slurred his voice.

Cicely sighed deeply and walked toward the door.

The Owner's office was bright and clean, every piece of

furniture set at a right angle to the objects around it. Behind his desk towered poster-sized photos of him and an older man with the mayor, the governor, congressmen. Another showed him coaching a Little League team, urging a young boy to round third base. Crisp blue ribbons from long-past county fairs hung amid the photos. He himself looked small, in pressed gray pants and a polka dot shirt, no tie. His features clustered toward the center of his face, his eyes sat way back in his head, and his nose crooked to the left. His complexion looked soft—Cicely doubted he had ever worked a day outdoors in his life. His mud-colored leather chair crinkled when he sat back down after greeting her.

"You work at the dance hall, don't you?" His skin held a deep tan, his face the color of freshly chopped wood. His shirt set off his darkened neck.

Cicely nodded. She didn't know if she should sit.

"I thought I recognized you," he said. "But you don't recognize me." He ran a hand over his thin blond hair. "I'm just another customer." He pressed the intercom and asked the secretary to bring two glasses of water. He pointed toward one of the chairs. "I love that place," he said as Cicely sat down. "Makes me think of old times, better times." The door opened and the secretary scurried in with the waters. "My grandfather built that building. That was the middle of nowhere back then—just sand and pine trees. They used to grow celery around there. Of course they can't grow anything anymore." It seemed to Cicely like he had already forgotten about her. His tone was even and dreamy. "He was a visionary." The ice in his glass tinkled as he gulped. "Although if somebody else hadn't invented air-conditioning this whole city would still just be woods, and my grandfather would have gone broke."

Just as he said that, the air-conditioning in the building clicked on and the vents erupted with a wash of cold air. The Owner howled with laughter.

Everyone always said the weather here was so great, but that was mostly because nobody ever went outside. The summers dragged on till Thanksgiving. At one point in her life, Cicely thought she could never live without air-conditioning. The idea of sleeping in the heat sounded beyond horrible. The first week in the house by the bay, she barely slept. She just lay there trying not to move, praying for it to get even a tiny bit cooler. It never did, but she learned to deal with it—the constant sweat, the great wet stillness of the humidity.

"My grandfather built the pier and the old downtown club, too, but most of what he put up is gone now." The Owner pointed out the window to a pair of pink buildings to the south, both of them just slightly shorter than the one they were in. "My own dad even knocked down a couple of his buildings to build those." He whistled. "I can only imagine what dinner conversation was like after that." He nodded toward the photographs on the wall. "The old man, that's him—my dad."

His look told her she was expected to respond. "He must be very powerful," she whispered.

"Because he got his photo taken with some politicians?" He shook his head. "All that takes is money." His face creased around his mouth and eyes when he smiled. "You know what I'd love to do? Knock down one of his buildings and replace it with something better."

What was this leading to? Cicely shifted in her seat and rested the glass of water on her thigh. The condensation left behind a cold wet circle. The breeze from the AC slipped into a small sliver of bare skin on her back, between her tank top and jeans. The afternoon had reached its zenith, and the colors in the window were violently alive. Way down below, she could see traffic flowing across the bridge and out to the Circle.

The Owner's expression turned sour. "But no. I'm stuck with nothing but a nest of shit, a bunch of half-built shit." He drained the last of his water. "Even if they do get finished, who will ever care? Nobody will care who built those Med Rev pieces of shit." He tipped back his chair slightly. "Nothing worth doing anymore."

Cicely guessed the Owner was forty, which made his dad, say, seventy. All these generations of men, hating one another.

The Owner leapt up and began pacing in a widening circle. He paused as he passed near her and leaned over, gripping the arms of her chair. "I hear things," he said, looking at his reflection in the shiny, cold floor, "about your father, too."

Cicely's first instinct was to spill everything, to throw all the blame toward her father. The air-conditioning, the view, this man's politeness—it all made it easy to think he was on her side. Would he hurt her father if she blamed him? Would he hurt her if she didn't? She covered her face with her hands and bent forward. Think. Think.

The Owner released his grip on her chair and resumed pacing. "Sometimes I wonder if I was just born in the wrong era," he said, more to the walls than to her. "But that's stupid. I wouldn't be myself. This body came into the world on a certain day and it will leave it on a certain day. There's no I to suck out, no I that could have lived any other time." He was framed in the window now, his body darkened by the bright light streaming in around him. The AC switched off and the room grew silent. "We're so miniscule. Ourselves, our families, our cities—we amount to so little. But we're here. We're here. You"—he pointed—"and I, together, in this room right now. What happens next matters."

"My father..." It just came out.

Her voice seemed to wake him up: "Where can we find him?"

"Day before yesterday... he left."

The Owner took two steps toward her. Two chains attached to the fan above gyrated and clacked into each other. "Where does he go?"

"The VFW."

One step closer. "What branch did he serve in? I was in Somalia."

She shook her head. "He fakes it, makes up stories to tell the other guys. They buy him beer."

Another step, and the Owner was at her side. He looked small behind his desk, but now he towered over her, his zipper right at eye level. Although it had been years, she remembered every detail of the mustache, Mike's mustache, the mustache of her manager at the Ponderosa, and the way he never cleaned it, just let the crumbs and grease accumulate, the way it seemed like a furry creature growing out of his nose. Recalling his smell, the scent of the deep fryer, cockroach traps, ammonia, made her shudder. She looked from the Owner's crotch up into his face, the angle menacing. He wore no mustache, but so close, she could see thick roots of hair just beginning to poke out from his cheeks. She glanced around the room. A pen sat on his desk, next to his keyboard. If he tried what Mike tried she would gladly stab out his eyes.

But he stepped back. "We'll need his name." He walked back behind his desk and sat down. "We'll find him."

Her body loosened. "And then…"

His fingers tapped at the keyboard. The screen was turned away from her, but she could see it come to life, lighting up his face with a gray metallic glow. "That's up to you."

17.

C.,

 I blame the hose.

 Do you remember that hose? I loved the feel of the grooves in my palms when I would water the flowers, how you could feel the rush of water, warm at first because it had been lying in the sun and then suddenly cool, and how it seemed to come to life in your hands, snapping upward and growing firm.

 When we first moved in, there was no hose. In fact, that might have been our first purchase together—your father and me. With no hose hooked up, the spigot in the back looked so sad and useless. We even splurged on that hose. There was a cheaper kind, with a thinner skin, but your father said it would puncture too easily, so we spent twice as much to get the nice kind. It even had some kind of feature that made it coil up on its own.

 In the evening, after dinner usually, I would go out in the backyard by myself and spray water. I loved being out there by myself. I started with the small flower bed on the left side, left if you were looking at the house from out back, then I sprayed along the fence on the left side where the bougainvilleas grew. I didn't use the *high water pressure, but the water would still kick up the soil, little flecks of dirt sticking to my ankles and calves. The hose would leave puddles in the dirt, but they'd drain away in moments. The plants were so thirsty.*

The nozzle was never perfectly sealed, so water would drip out of the metal rings where it attached to the hose and onto my wrists. The chill felt so good on summer evenings. I didn't wear shoes because I liked the feel of water between my toes so much, even with the scratch of that awful crabgrass that grew in our backyard. I used to stand there holding the hose, just staring at the sky. In my memory, it was always orange, orange and pink and red, and there was a telephone post in the back left corner, the lines drooping and connecting and crossing, somehow making the sky even more beautiful—rigid wires in the foreground, burning clouds in the background. I tried to take photos of the sky one evening but when I got the prints back—this was when people still got prints—it looked pathetic, flat. I didn't even keep the pictures. They depressed me too much.

The noises. They just rushed back at me while I was writing these words. The bugs, yes, the crickets and cicadas, but also the rustle of squirrels chasing one another along branches, the kids splashing in the pool down the street, the spigot's whine.

And then you stepped on a nail. I'm sure you remember. You were thirteen, fourteen? You came out back to ask me about your homework, a math problem. There were a few loose boards stacked up outside and you jumped up on them. I'll never forget your scream. I was sure you were dying. I dropped the hose, but because I had clipped the handle closed, it just kept on spraying and spraying, straight up into the air, like a sprinkler.

I almost fainted when I saw the nail sticking up through your foot. It had jabbed through your whole foot, maybe an inch or so back from where your toes started. There wasn't much blood, not yet, but I remember the brown tip of the nail. I could tell right away it was rusty and flaky. You just kept screaming and screaming and screaming. The neighbors, I'm sure, thought someone was being murdered.

I yelled for your father. It took him forever to come outside. My first thought was to pull out the nail, but then I thought that just might make it worse. I didn't know what to do. Your father and I argued. He was annoyed I was even asking for help. "It's a nail," he kept saying, like it was no big thing.

The board the nail was attached to was wet and old and eaten away. Your father put a boot next to your foot and bent the wood up to break it off. The nail stayed in, but now there was just a small wedge of board underneath your foot.

By then, the blood had really begun flowing. Your father scooped you up and walked next door. The guy who lived there let us use his truck every now and then. But I couldn't budge. I just stood there watching the scene like it was part of a movie. Your father explained things to the guy next door then took his keys and drove off to the hospital. I knew I should go with you, but I couldn't. I was frozen. I just stood there, getting soaked by the hose, which was still spouting water over half the yard.

By the time I walked over to the spigot and turned off the water, it had grown dark, and lights were flicking on up and down the street. I left the hose where it was, snaked out across the lawn, and peeled off my clothes inside. I didn't want to do anything but go to bed.

You and your father came back a few hours later. You were fine. You just needed a tetanus shot and some bandages.

In the morning, after you went off to school, I stared out the window at the hose, still lying deep down in the grass. That very morning, I went out and bought one of those round plastic things you attach to a house to wind up your hose on. But even after I screwed it in and pulled up the hose and everything looked clean and neat again, it didn't feel right. That night, instead of watering any flowers or plants, I just stood there, staring at the coiled hose and the small wet stain that accumulated on the concrete from the slow drip, drip, drip of the nozzle.

M.

It wasn't a math problem she had gone out to ask her mother about. It was a book report she had to write—a page or two on *Nineteen Eighty-Four*. Her father hadn't read it, thought it was dumb to name a book after a year, so he told her to leave him alone and go ask her mom. But she hadn't read it, either.

The next day, Cicely explained to her teacher why she hadn't done the report and threatened to pull off her shoe and show him the rank bandages if he didn't believe her. She limped around school for a week before the wound started to heal.

Cicely put down the letter and leaned over to look at her foot. A small, round white scar still showed where the nail had punctured her. She thought of her father, and the nail that had entered his foot just the other day. She didn't remember that her mother didn't come with them to the ER. Everything from the jump to when they pulled out the nail was a blur.

Since her father had disappeared, Cicely hadn't checked to see if the first letter from her mother was still hidden underneath her mattress. She bolted up the steps, two at a time. The letter was gone. Her father must have stolen that, as well. Which meant he knew she had heard from her, and he knew her mother's Orlando PO number, too. Three letters she had received—now she had only one. Monday was garbage day, but Sunday was really garbage day. Was that how the first letter began?

The money her father had stolen would have been more than enough for a bus ticket to Orlando and a place to flop for a week. Did her father set out to find her mother? Cicely didn't want him to locate her first, before she could. More than that, she wanted the Owner to find him and inflict pain.

Cicely walked toward the hole in the wall, her hiding spot. The man with the box cutter had ripped out all the insulation. It looked like cotton candy strewn about. She gathered together all the loose pieces and held them out the window. The wind ripped them from her hand; the pink tufts danced away in the breeze.

A few drops of blood stained the floor where the man with the box cutter had held her against the wall. She walked to the bathroom to get napkins to clean it up. She had forgotten about her shit, the one she had taken while the man with the box cutter waited downstairs. The smell seemed even worse than before; it had a sharp undercurrent of rotting radishes. Flies swarmed around the toilet. The scene nauseated her, but she knew she couldn't stay in the house unless she dealt with it. From downstairs she found the bucket that wasn't for drinking and tossed its fuzzy water in the bushes then refilled it from the bay. Upstairs, she stripped down to her underwear. Kneeling in front of the toilet, she very nearly vomited. She shooed away the flies and then very slowly poured the water from the bucket onto the green and gray turds piled up in the bowl. The shit slid down into the plumbing. She replaced the bucket downstairs and scrubbed her hands with a moist bar of blue soap. The blood. She still had to clean up the blood. She spit on a napkin and scrubbed at the crusted drops on the floor upstairs. They came up easily.

The Owner had told her to stay there, not to worry about paying any more rent till they found her father, but the house felt enormous with no one else around. Cicely stood outside and looked at the home. The Owner was right. Even if it was finished one day, it would be ugly. The details that had been completed, the ocher-colored roof tiles and the curlicued molding that lined the front, already looked ridiculous—dated and fake.

18.

Cicely sat there watching Zinnia get ready for her show.

Zinnia slipped into her sparkly dress and pulled the straps over her shoulders. "You didn't come in last night," she said.

"Some kind of bug. I was in bed all day."

Zinnia combed her hair. With each tug, her white curls sprang up higher than before. "Nothing to do with our thing, right?"

Could the placentas somehow make her sick? Zinnia said there was no danger transporting them, but Cicely hadn't considered whether handling the bags might be hazardous. "Like, they made me sick?"

"Not sick sick. Nerves. Stress."

Cicely waved a hand. "Oh no. It has nothing to do with that."

Zinnia rubbed on lipstick and popped her lips. A smudge stuck to her front teeth. She wiped it away with a Kleenex. When she did her makeup, she bent right up to the mirror. She told Cicely the lights onstage revealed every little imperfection. She needed to be precise.

The back door banged open and in walked Delanna. She giggled. "Hope I'm not interrupting anything." She tossed her purse in her chair and started to change her clothes. Cicely had never noticed the small peach-colored scar that cut sideways just above her right kneecap.

"The fuck does that mean?" Cicely asked.

As she unhooked her bra, Delanna shrugged.

Zinnia lit a cigarette. Smoking was part of her preshow

routine. She told Cicely she liked the way a recent smoke made her throat feel when she sang, that it gave her an extra rumble on the low notes that she couldn't do without. Her brow tightened as she glared at Delanna.

"It's just…" Delanna thought for a moment. "Everyone knows."

Did people think Cicely and Zinnia were lesbians? Cicely opened her mouth to say something but shut it without a squeak. Better that than them suspecting the truth.

"Delanna," Zinnia said, "keep your mouth shut." She took a puff.

An anxious laugh shook out of Delanna's throat. "OK. Whatever."

Zinnia hardened. She took the burning cigarette between her thumb and forefinger and pointed its orange tip toward Delanna. Delanna's back was to her, but she watched Zinnia nervously in the mirror.

"Delanna…" Zinnia's voice turned soft. She looked at the ash accumulating at the end of her cigarette. "If I ever hear you talking shit about either me or Cicely…"

As Delanna turned around to face Zinnia, she dropped her lip gloss. Cicely enjoyed her fear.

"You're crazy," Delanna said. She hurriedly put away her things and scurried to the door, looking back at Cicely, whose face lit up with obscene amusement. "Crazy."

Zinnia jabbed the cigarette in Delanna's direction and Delanna, spooked, slammed the door behind her. Zinnia and Cicely both burst out laughing.

19.

Days passed. There was no news of her father, no contact from the Owner. It surprised Cicely how easily she slipped into life on her own. She didn't have to order double when she brought home food from the hall, didn't have to wash anyone else's clothes, didn't have to make sure she was dressed before she went downstairs in the morning. Even the smell of the dead fish seemed to bother her less.

On Tuesday, her day off, she skipped Father Bill's sermon and took the bus to the library. She thumbed the spines of CDs she had loved in high school: Joni Mitchell, *Oar*, Leonard Cohen. She wished she could hear them again, but her Discman had malfunctioned long ago. Perhaps Goodwill had a used one—she'd have to check. She wondered if Zinnia had made any records—she'd have to ask.

It took her an hour to pick a couple books to check out. The selection was so much smaller than it had been when she used to come with her mother. To her childish eyes, the library had been enormous. Shelf after shelf loomed over her. Now it looked shabby and rundown, with a paltry offering, and there was only one librarian on duty. When Cicely asked her for a recommendation, she just snapped a gum bubble and pointed to the shelf displaying the most recent titles, which were not recent at all. The three books Cicely eventually found were all mysteries. When she was younger, she loved thrillers set in foreign countries. The plots were fun, but more than that she loved the strange foods the detectives and criminals ate, the drinks they shared, the peculiar architecture of their cities.

That evening, she sat outside and read, leaning against the rocks piled up behind the house. When the sun melted away and she could no longer make out the words on the page, she put on her lemon dress and strolled to the Circle. Light from the stores made the sidewalks glow; mannequins draped in glittering fabrics contorted themselves in shop windows. Cicely had had a few decent nights at the hall, so she splurged on mint ice cream. As the scoop melted, she licked the sugary juice from her fingers, then crunched into the griddled cone. The chilled water she gulped down afterward was the freshest, coldest water she had tasted in years. She smacked her frigid lips as she walked the Circle for a second time, eying dresses she could never afford, reviewing menus she would never sample.

The stink from the fish had receded for the day, and couples in bright prints walked to and fro, their arms linked behind backs. Women's heels clopped on the pavement. Sweet tobacco drifted from men's cigars. Crab legs cracked between metal pincers. It wasn't cool, not at all, but it felt like it might be, as if the end of summer were in sight at last. Cicely stood outside one bar, basted with neon glare, and watched frozen drinks tumble in a row of canisters set into the wall behind the counter. As she watched, customers came and went, each swing of the door releasing notes from the digital jukebox inside. She pressed her fingertips to the tall glass that faced the street. The window was warm. Its tiny vibrations slithered inside her.

20.

Driving to the tower from the hospital the next night, she had already made up her mind: she would open the bag. Before she placed it in the cooler, she had checked the seal, actually three seals—three threaded strips like at the top of a sandwich bag. Once those seals were zipped up, the top third of the package was then folded in half and taped tightly. She could peel back the tape and replace it later and Zinnia would never notice. She hadn't said a word about the package Cicely had let fall to the ground.

"Do they cook them, or just eat them raw?" Cicely had asked. Zinnia didn't answer. If they cooked them, there would be recipes, if there were recipes, there were likely meals, feasts that used placentas from start to finish, tasting menus, aficionados, connoisseurs. Zinnia said it wasn't like that, that the doula's customers ate them for their health, that they were mostly mothers who had eaten their own placentas after giving birth and then gotten hooked.

"Did you try it?" Cicely asked. "Did you taste it?"

"She made me."

When she got to the tower, Cicely plopped the bag down on the cot and clicked on the bare bulb overhead. The bag was maybe three feet by two. On her knees, she tugged gently at the tape, trying not to rip it. When it finally popped loose, she cracked the first two seals, held her breath, and slowly opened the third and final seal. She expected a huge whiff of blood to come rushing at her, but nothing happened right away. With the mouth of the package now a wide open O, she leaned in and tried to look inside. But the bulb overhead was weak, and the interior of the bag remained a purple void. She leaned in further, pinching the plastic and pulling up. Mouth closed, she pulled in a huge breath. Metal and rot—that was all she could smell—metal and rot. As the scent sucked down into her lungs, her torso shook. She slipped backward, onto her butt.

The dark circle at the end of the bag collapsed into a horizontal slit. The smell now was all around her. Cicely scampered to her feet and banged her head on the lightbulb, which began to swing violently, throwing terrible shadows around the room. The bulb brushed and singed Cicely's cheek. She tossed her head to the side at the burn. She stilled the bulb by grabbing the metal cord and cranked open the tower's four tall windows. As the smell dissipated, Cicely tenderly resealed the bag and taped it back up. The fridge made a kissing sound as she opened the door and tucked away the placentas. She didn't see how she could ever take a bite of that.

It was late—almost two a.m.—but she could still hear music and chatter from the village's lone restaurant. She needed out.

Unemployed fishermen still wearing their rubber overalls and boots leered at her as she walked toward the restaurant. She clutched a small tube of rolled-up cash in her pocket and made sure to look left, right, and behind every few steps. She had been robbed once. It would not happen again.

The bar was about half-full. Most of the patrons had separated into couples, but in the corner one long table offered refuge to a large group of men and women—the men in shabby secondhand suits and ties whose knots had been pulled loose, the women in colorful tight-fitting dresses. Empty pitchers crowded the table. Cicely guessed they were celebrating a wedding. Despite the village's decline, its residents still approached special occasions with debauched reverence. It wasn't a proper wedding unless a whole crowd of naked fishermen was splashing around in the surf when the sun came up.

One woman at the table sat in a man's lap, her arms draped

around his neck. He was crooning a wordless tune, and she drank it in. Another couple got up to dance. They stepped on each other's feet and laughed and swayed and the woman rested her head against the man's chest. One of the other guys joined in the song, and then another, and pretty soon the whole table was singing the melody. Cicely slurped ginger ale through a bendable red straw, watching. Her shoulders waved back and forth with the song. It sounded nothing like Zinnia's music, more folky, but it felt similar. At the end of the tune, everyone applauded, even those who weren't part of the wedding. The man who began the singalong stood and bowed. He winked at Cicely.

Where were the bride and groom? It was a village custom that a newly married couple spend their honeymoon on a houseboat, puttering up and down the Intracoastal. The residents believed that by spending the first days of their marriage together on the water, they weren't just committing to each other, they were committing to the sea, displaying love for the tides that gave them life. Cicely had often seen the boat, spray-painted with lustful messages by generations of fishermen, floating in the bay or passing beneath the bridge near home. Inside, unseen, the couple embraced. Cicely always pictured the women with curvy hips and manes of red hair in emerald swimsuits that made them look like mermaids, and the men in black T-shirts that hid auburn torsos, dry and caked from years on the water.

Cicely never thought much about being married herself. She fantasized, of course—about a man who lived with her in her condo and painted the walls and fixed the garbage disposal— but the object of her fantasy always remained dreamlike, unreal, as if she could see him standing there in a black suit but his face remained forever blurry, like in TV shows about criminals when they showed the obscured faces of victims. What the man might say, what he might enjoy doing, how he would make love to her—she could never pin down those details.

She had been attracted to men over the years, of course, and had flirted with them and even gone on a few dates, but over time they always grew ugly. Or did she feel ugly about them? Sometimes, when she considered the world and hated it, it became impossible to tell if it deserved her hate or if the world simply reflected a hate radiating out from within her. At some point—it happened gradually, without her knowing it—she had given up trying to answer that riddle.

She munched on ice. The wedding party was breaking up. Men and women kissed and giggled and rubbed against each other. Some skipped outside. It hurt to see people happy. Cicely left two bucks on the bar and walked outside. The moon looked like a giant shimmering coin, bright enough to leave shadows rustling along the ground. As she walked back to the tower, every row of bushes concealed the fumbled groans of love.

21.

A fourth letter came to her at the dance hall the next night.

> C.,
>
> *I'm trying to explain myself. But as the words pile up, the truth seems farther away than it did when I began.*
>
> *The simple fact is that I told your father I hated him and he gave me two choices: you or me. I could either stay and take care of you or I could go. You couldn't go with me. I chose to save myself.*
>
> *For years I tried to convince myself it wasn't that simple, that there were other factors. Your father threatened me. That helped me sleep some. But the truth is I chose me over you. I'm sure you know that, even if you don't know that.*
>
> *Did your father tell you anything? Did he tell you I was dead? Kidnapped? Locked up? I can only guess that he began poisoning you the day I left.*
>
> *When I told him I hated him he assumed I had been sleeping around. "When?" I asked him. "When would I possibly have time to sleep around?" Once you started school I found that job taking tolls on the highway. I made breakfast and lunch for both of you before I went to work and when I came home I made dinner for both*

of you. What time did I have for an affair? My lunch break? I just laughed at him, which only made him angrier. I tried to reason with him, but I could tell he just thought I was making excuses, trying to hide something.

It must have been hard for him to understand. It wasn't like the movies, where everybody has a reason for how they feel—something that happened to them that explains how they behave. How could I explain it was the hose? It made no sense. But that didn't stop me from feeling it. Everything in our home repulsed me. Everything felt heavy, like it was pressing down on my shoulders, like I was carrying around our kitchen cabinets strapped to my back. We didn't really have all that much compared to other folks—we didn't even have a car—but it seemed like we owned all this stuff, garbage, and that it was up to me to tote it around all day.

I was twenty when I met your father, on the beach. I was home from college for the summer and went to the beach by myself every evening. One Saturday he was there with some friends from the factory. He was so good-looking. His T-shirt seemed like the most beautiful T-shirt I'd ever seen, and he had nice muscles from work. That first time, he came right over and offered me a beer and a sandwich and invited me to come hang out with him and his friends. I took the beer but said no to hanging out. "Next time come alone," I told him, and he did. The following Saturday we walked back into the mangroves and made out in the sand and after that we just kept meeting up.

I thought of him as a townie, someone I could have a fling with during summer break, *and he knew that, probably resented it, but he wasn't complaining, either. He told me he loved my ankles. He seemed so tender, so loving. I didn't want to marry him, didn't want to get stuck at home, but I thought he would make a very nice husband for someone else. And then a week before I was set to go back to Tallahassee I found out I was pregnant.*

Did we have to get married? Probably not. But something inside made me feel like this was destiny. I was so childish. I thought I was meant to have this life. Any life is as good as another, I thought, if you embrace it and live it. I could be a housewife. I could forget about marine biology. I could change diapers and feed my husband and soak stains.

I failed. A loving mother never would have left.

Do you remember one morning when I couldn't stop crying at the breakfast table? When you saw me you looked shocked. You were wearing your black boots with the pink laces—I loved those. You asked me what happened and I told you I was sad. "Why?" you asked. "Just work stuff," I said. I wanted to think of a better lie. You knew I was being untruthful, but you seemed to accept it. But did you know?

M.

Cicely remembered the morning and yes, she knew her mother had lied to her. At that age, she already knew her father was a loser. She refolded the letter and held it in her lap. The bus was playing another comedy, *Genital Warts and All*, but the sound was off. The cheap fabric of the seats scratched at her elbows.

It was difficult to picture her father as attractive. The letter suggested that at one point he was attentive, loving, affectionate—characteristics Cicely rarely saw. They had their fun playing cards, yes, but even though he would laugh and tell stories Cicely knew her presence was incidental, that he would have been just as happy unspooling his tales to a complete stranger. He never asked her how her job was going, didn't seem to care if she came home depressed or angry—as long as she had dinner.

But the letter inspired a new anger, too, at her mother. He had given her a choice and she had chosen to save herself. Did she even try to fight him? Did she call the cops? She could have snuck away with Cicely. He never would have found them.

The bus screeched to a halt. A kid wearing basketball shorts climbed on board. Headphones hugged his skull, their cord drooping down below his waist and then back up into his right pocket. He plopped into the seat right in front of Cicely. Maybe seventeen years old, Cicely guessed. His head must have been recently clipped—the back of his neck was shaved clean and the edge of his auburn hair crossed from left to right in a perfectly straight line.

Cicely enjoyed a well-cut head of men's hair. When she was a kid, her mother cut her father's hair with clippers from Goodwill. She zipped up and down his scalp, not bothering to adjust the plastic guard. A spiky fur covered his head in those days. With Cicely, she'd use scissors, cutting a straight horizontal line in the back and above her eyes; for years, Cicely's only hairstyle was flat bangs. But one year, for her birthday, Cicely asked for a real haircut, like the ones her friends got, and she and her mother took the bus to a modest salon, where they sat Cicely in a big puffy pink vinyl chair and washed her hair carefully, massaging her head and winding a hot, wet towel into a circle over her face. Cicely had never felt prettier, but the stylish cut faded over the months that followed. Before long she was just herself again.

The kid with the sharp hair got off at her stop.

"Nice haircut," Cicely said as the two of them stepped out onto the pavement.

He gave her a quizzical look then lifted his headphones from his ears. "What did you say?" She felt his contempt.

"Nice haircut." She enunciated.

"Yeah OK," he said. His headphones snapped back over his ears. As he turned from her and took off in the direction opposite her own, he snorted snot back into his throat and spit onto the hot concrete.

22.

The rumble from the truck woke her up before dawn. She knew the sound immediately—the man with the box cutter. At first she thought he had come for her. Had her deal with the Owner expired? In those first confused moments after waking, all she could see was the cut on her arm, the hot blood dripping down inside her elbow. She felt her head banging against the wall all over again. She looked around for something sharp, but her only knife was downstairs. No way she could get to the kitchen before he saw her. The window. Could she jump? She hurried to the opening. Too high. No trees to grab onto, no drainpipes within reach.

The roar from the truck ceased. She heard voices. The man with the box cutter wasn't alone.

"Cicely!" It was a bark, but not an authoritative one. In another life, she might have considered it friendly. "Cicely!" Imploring, but still not demanding.

She wrapped herself in an old faded red robe and walked downstairs. It was way dark out, but she recognized her father immediately. He was down on his knees, bent forward in the dust. Cicely gasped when he looked up and she saw his face, bruised and swollen, with blood crusted on his cheeks and underneath his nose, which angled to the left in a way that it had not before. His shirt, a new-looking guayabera, was ripped at the collar. Thin cuts criss-crossed his legs. He tried to stand up, but his knees were raw, caked with blood and dirt, and they buckled under his weight. He wheezed as if something liquid were trapped in his lungs. She wanted to feel pity when she saw him, but all she could find was satisfaction. He had finally suffered.

The man with the box cutter stood a few yards behind her father. The box cutter was in his hand, its pale blade extended. He coughed. "He was crashing with one of the regulars from the VFW. All I had to do was mention a name and that he made up every story he ever told. They were happy to point me in the right direction."

Her father's uglied face showed it hadn't been quite that easy. His eyes brimmed with tears as he looked up at her.

"He spent all the money."

"Papa." She kneeled in front of him and took his hands. They were rough and dry, with deep cracks that Cicely traced with her fingertips. "Papa." His face looked even uglier up close: the ring around his left eye had turned purple.

"Cicely." His voice battled with the breeze. He cleared his throat. "I…"

Her tone was hard: "What."

His lips wiggled.

"What."

A whoosh of helicopter blades sounded over the bay. Silver clouds crept from the skyline out toward the island. The air smelled like batteries.

He couldn't even apologize. Even if he didn't mean it, he couldn't even fake it and apologize. He had stolen from her, had robbed her, had lived off her work for years, had insulted her, had cursed her, had yelled at her. She had long ago given up hope of hearing the truth; she at least deserved a lie.

Cicely backed away and pulled her robe tight, gripping her torso. There was nothing left inside but rage. She pictured herself at age fifteen, in the weeks after her mother left. She tried to keep her normal life going: she woke up on time for school, tied her pink bootlaces on the bus, and turned in her homework. But when she came home there was no food, the clothes that had been piled on the carpet hadn't budged, the flickering light bulb in the bathroom hadn't been replaced, and her father, he barely moved, sitting amid greasy takeout boxes and empty sixers of Busch, staring at the TV during those rare moments when he deigned to open his eyes and consider the room around him. A couple weeks later, the factory sent him a letter informing him that he was terminated, and then the late notices from the bank started piling up in the mailbox, and pretty soon those late notices became foreclosure notices. But still nothing made him budge. Cicely thought he would get back on his feet—it was just a matter of time. How stupid. That fifteen-year-old, what had she been feeling? Guilt. The tug of responsibility. Faith that the man who helped create her would feel the same. That he would eventually come around. That he was just going through a tough time. Cicely screamed silently at that fifteen-year-old. She should have gotten out, too. Her mother's disappearance should have been a clue. This family meant nothing.

And if she had crept up one night when he was passed out on the couch. If she had quietly taken the peeling knife, the one with the curved blade, and snuck up on him sleeping and put the blade to his throat and demanded all the money that was left. If she had done that?

"The rent remains outstanding," the man with the box cutter said. "The Owner is giving you two options. Add to your debt and keep paying it off. Or we take him and we're even through the end of the year."

"Take him where?"

"A project."

Cicely frowned.

"A golf course. He'll be fine. If he behaves."

She nodded. "OK."

Her father moaned. Cicely could see the hope leave him.

The night air felt like a hot bath, but everything inside Cicely ran cold. She leaned over and stroked her father's face. No one had shaved him, and his cheeks were prickly and gray. She held him tightly and kissed him full on his dry, flaking lips. His breath tasted of acid and bile. He tried to wrap his arms around her legs as she stood up, but she was too quick. She stepped to the man with the box cutter and reached for his blade. He hesitated, but his grip on the box cutter loosened. It was suddenly in her hands. She squeezed the blue plastic handle as she walked up behind her father. His guayabera was streaked with dirt and stained yellow with beer. The flesh above his shirt collar was pink. Her father was still kneeling, and his head was just level with her waist. Using her left hand, she pushed his skull forward, exposing more of his neck. With her right hand, she pressed the rusty blade into his skin and made three quick slashes—something like a scraggly letter C. The cut wasn't deep, but her father cried out and wiggled away. He flopped forward onto the ground and flipped over and raised his hands to defend himself. Cicely tossed the bloody instrument into the dirt and kicked dust toward her father. Without looking back, she walked into their home, her home, and climbed the stairs. After the truck doors slammed shut and the engine howled to life, Cicely heard it peel out onto the street that led back to the bridge, back toward downtown. She slept without dreams.

Part Two

23.

August melted into September. The weather should have cooled, but it didn't, and no rain came to flush the humidity. Even the nights remained moist. Taking a stroll left Cicely drenched and lethargic.

She moved in with Zinnia. She packed what little she had into a cardboard box she pilfered from work and caught the bus to the fishing village. Zinnia's home was just minutes from the tower. A house, a small, squarish unit with windows and running water, set atop short brick pillars that kept it from touching the ground—a flood precaution. The home had a long galley kitchen in the back and two small bedrooms that both connected to the structure's sole bathroom. The wood floors, original, squeaked under Cicely's feet as she lugged in her box. The clatter of the AC wall unit thrilled her. She dumped her stuff on the floor and stood in front of the cold flow, drinking it in. She slowly turned the temperature dial down to its lowest setting, just to see how cold it could get.

After Cicely put her box in the room Zinnia had set aside for her, she poked her head into Zinnia's bedroom. It was the only room in the house that had carpet—thick and red and soft—and it smelled of tobacco. Zinnia's bed wasn't much of a bed, just a mattress and a box spring. Her sheets were disheveled, pulled back and twisted, and her pillow looked like it had been choked. To the left of the bed stood a dresser with half its drawers pulled out. Its edge was nicked and beaten, like the dressers of guys Cicely knew in high school, guys who used the edges of drawers and counters as leverage to pop tops off beer bottles. Touching the dresser lightly, Cicely peered into the open drawers. She saw old jeans, T-shirts, a few strands of plastic jewels. Behind her, on the floor near the bed, lay a wrinkled paperback edition of *The Awakening*, which Cicely had read in tenth grade, her last full year in school.

Shamed by her peeping, Cicely tiptoed out of Zinnia's room and into hers. It was still filled with old instruments and equipment Zinnia had collected—most of it looked like it hadn't been touched in years. Dust had collected on cymbals and in the grooves of fretboards. The zither Zinnia had played for Cicely so many nights ago leaned in the corner. Cicely's bed didn't have a box spring, but after years of sleeping near the floor, she didn't care. She didn't have a dresser, either, so she piled her folded clothes in neat stacks along the wall.

The skinny bathroom that connected her room to Zinnia's seemed palatial to Cicely. A cream-colored plastic tub sat in a recess to the left, opposite a long counter with two teal sinks. Cicely turned the hot water knobs till they halted. Scalding water flooded out and the mirror filled with condensation.

The house didn't have much of a backyard. The ground was coated with jagged white seashells. Sea grapes clawed their way out of the earth along the perimeter. The one luxury: a ropey old hammock that clung to the trunks of two oak trees anchored in the corners of the yard. The hammock creaked when Cicely hopped up into it; the trees groaned. She eased onto her back and looked up through the branches. But the dead fish smell was particularly bad that day. In no time she was coughing up green mucus and crying peppery tears. Shells crackled under her sandals as she scurried back to the safety of the AC.

24.

The hall was hosting a candidates' forum for the five men running for the county planning commission, and the interior had been decked out in red, white, and blue bunting for the occasion. Banners with names and slogans and party affiliations dangled from the rafters, and a long banquet table had been set up onstage. The manager of the hall asked Zinnia to do sound for the event, and she spent the afternoon snaking thick black cords from the amplifiers in back through the legs of the table and up behind the frilly decorations strung along the table's edge. She connected the cords to the microphones set out in front of the candidates' chairs and wormed another over to the podium where the moderator would stand and pose questions. In the quiet hour before her shift started, Cicely sat and watched Zinnia work.

None of the names on the flyer promoting the forum sounded familiar to Cicely, but she recognized each of the men when they arrived for soundcheck. They were all regulars. The hue of their suits ranged from cobalt to navy, the color of their ties from scarlet to crimson. Small pins bearing the Florida state flag adorned their lapels. "Good evening," each of them intoned into a mic. "It's great to be here." Zinnia—dressed in all black, even a black cap, to hide herself—fiddled with knobs on her mixing board and nodded when things sounded all right. The candidates had all produced videos to introduce themselves. Their aides plugged laptops into the hall's video system and tested out the clips. They all looked the same to Cicely: high-contrast images of waving flags, the Everglades, flying birds, the capitol. She had never voted.

After the tests, the men walked back to the girls' dressing room, which had been commandeered for the evening. They sat for makeup, met with consultants, and went over final preparations as the hall filled with what Cicely guessed constituted the voting public. It was a quiet audience. Attendees populated the tables in an orderly fashion, sipped their Mai Tais, and chatted. No one yelled at Cicely for more drinks and no one slapped the red, white, and blue tassels attached to her pasties.

Cicely's stomach dropped when she saw the Owner walk in. Although he had told her he was a hall regular, she hadn't seen him since their talk in his office.

Five or six men and women at tables near the door rose to greet him, pumping his hand and slapping him on the back or leaning in to kiss him on the cheek. His face and neck were just as tan as before; his pale pink shirt looked freshly cleaned and pressed. He smiled broadly and nodded at each table as he waded through the tightly packed chairs, eventually finding a solitary open seat at a table near the front. Everyone else at the table rose to greet him. He circled the table, grasping hands, kissing, hugging. It looked like a family reunion. When he was finally seated, he took a deep breath and drank from the Mai Tai in front of him and surveyed the room. His eyes found Cicely's and a small grin conveyed recognition. He raised a palm, a quarter-wave. Cicely smiled back then busied herself refilling waters and Mai Tais. Only a few minutes remained before the debate began, and everyone wanted a fresh round.

Applause broke out when the five men filed onstage and sat behind the table. A blond newswoman whom Cicely recognized followed the candidates, and the applause increased. She took her place behind the podium and smiled in fake shyness, as if she couldn't understand the attention. Eventually, the clapping ceased, and the newswoman introduced herself and the candidates and explained the format.

The hall manager had instructed the waitresses to cease

service as soon as the debate started so as not to make any noise. Cicely wandered back behind the riser in the rear of the hall, where a few television cameras were mounted. Dwayne, Delanna, Hilda, and other staffers all gathered around too, whispering to one another and ignoring the debate. Cicely didn't care to listen, either, but she hoped the candidates sounded good, for Zinnia's sake.

Bored, she walked outside. Vans with TV news logos idled in the parking lot. Satellite dishes pointed out into the night sky. Rope-thick cables crossed the pavement and into the hall through a propped-open window. Cicely strolled to the east, where the grass was coated in the on-off blink of the hall's lurid sign. Her heels sunk into the soft muck of the embankment as she climbed toward the Interstate. When she reached concrete, she turned around and looked behind her. Even though she wasn't high up, the city was flat enough that she could see the skyscrapers downtown. In between grew strip malls, chain stores, fast food joints, pet shops—the dark night broken up by the occasional streetlight.

A car sped by, leaving a trail of wind that gusted up Cicely's bare back. Turning around, Cicely rested her hands on the rough gray guardrail that blocked off the highway. A Maybach roared by, a sharp honk-honk puncturing the night. Just then did Cicely remember that only pasties covered her nipples. She waited for another car to pass, wondering if she'd earn any more honks, but none came. The Interstate was deserted. She trudged back down the embankment and toward the TV vans.

"You gentlemen need anything?" she asked, leaning into the open back door of one of the vans. Two guys sat in front of a bank of monitors, their fingers on keyboards and their necks craned toward the screens. They shushed her.

Enjoying the moist air on her skin, Cicely wandered over to the rectangular retention pond dug into the ground on the hall's north side. Styrofoam cups and empty bags of chips floated on the surface; brown muck collected in the corner near the drain. Were they saying anything inside about how ugly they had made this world? Probably not. Where they lived, all this was kept far away, out of view. But they couldn't ignore the fish, the fish that kept washing up faster than the county could remove them. What did they have to say about that? Cicely wished she had stuck around inside and listened.

The hall doors burst open and the crowd streamed out, Cicely's cue that she needed to go bus tables. She navigated upstream, against the people leaving. Just inside the door, Cicely ran smack into a man hurrying out. She looked up to apologize. It was the Owner.

"I'm, I'm sorry," she said. "Excuse me."

His teeth looked so white as he responded: "No problem, Miss, no problem at all." One of his paws came to rest on her shoulder. He squeezed her gently and then passed.

The other waitresses sneered at Cicely for being late to help. Half the tables had already been cleared by the time Cicely grabbed a black rubber tub and started filling it with dirty glasses. It took about an hour to remove all the stemware and replace the tablecloths. Zinnia broke down all the AV supplies, packing them away in black crates and wheeling them to the storage room behind the stage. When they had both changed back into their regular clothes and clocked out, Cicely and Zinnia hugged.

"How'd everything go?" Cicely asked.

"You didn't listen?" Zinnia twirled her keys on her finger as they crossed the parking lot to the van. Cicely shook her head. "Oh," Zinnia said, drawing out the vowel, "fine, fine."

Together, they drove home.

25.

The first tingle of pain in the back of the throat told Cicely she was getting sick. In an hour, the mucus began to flow, and Cicely found herself swallowing and snorting to clear her throat. An hour after that, her head dizzied when she stood up and her limbs and shoulders ached. She tried to get ready to go to work, but she knew she couldn't make it. She asked Zinnia to tell the manager she wouldn't be in and then crawled back into bed, shivering and cold despite the heat. She hated her job, but she still felt as if she was letting down the manager; she hadn't missed a shift in at least a year.

That evening, she snored, and when she came to, her pillow was soaked with a revolting mix of drool, snot, and sweat—she flipped over the pillow and wiped her face with a shirt she found on the floor.

Zinnia brought home Tylenol from work and fed them to her in the morning. Cicely hadn't eaten dinner the night before but she wasn't hungry at all, just achingly thirsty. Zinnia held a glass of cold water to Cicely's lips and rubbed Cicely's scalp through her hair, humming one of her tunes. The room grew fuzzy.

Alone, Cicely masturbated. Whenever she got sick, the urge hit her with force. Was it just boredom from being confined to bed? Just simple pleasure when her body hurt?

The orgasm seemed to wake her up; she felt energetic enough to wander out to the kitchen. Zinnia had gone out, but she had left two tea bags dunked in a pot of water on the cold stove. Cicely flipped on the burner and waited for the tea to warm, bobbing the bags up and down and dragging them across the surface of the water. When it was ready she squeezed in a jot of honey and the juice from a wedge of lemon and went back to bed. The tea was scalding, so she set the cup on the floor and masturbated again. Coming was a reprieve from the pain. She found her place in one of the mysteries she had borrowed from the library, began reading, and brought the hot cup to her lips.

26.

The next day, with Cicely still laid up, Zinnia told her the story of how she grew up.

Her dad was a musician, that Cicely knew. What she didn't know was that to make ends meet he hunted feral hogs on one of the big spreads out east. For generations, the land had belonged to the Wilson family, pioneers who moved south to Florida after the Indian Removal Act and got rich growing celery. But Hurricane Easy drowned half the county's land and annihilated the Wilsons' harvest, pushing the family into tourism instead. While they opened hotels and condos on the barrier islands, their spread deteriorated, choked with air potatoes and melaleuca. Much later, their condos went bust, and the family, again strapped for cash, sold development rights to the county, which pledged to restore the land and rid it of invasive species. But during the decades of disuse, feral hogs had taken over. When a county team armed with herbicides drove out onto the prairie, a family of hogs attacked and overturned their ATV. The wreck trapped one of the men and snapped his spine while the hogs tore at the arms and legs of the others. Only one survived.

To counter the hogs, the county issued rifles to anyone willing to patrol the prairie and offered a cash reward. Every couple weeks, Zinnia's father packed up enough gear and food for a few days and caught a ride out to the old farm with a group of musician buddies. During the day, they shot every hog they could find and chopped off their ears to prove to the county how many they'd killed, and at night they built giant bonfires and jammed. Zinnia's father riffed on a glockenspiel while the other hunters traded instruments and improvised. Sometimes they'd bring along a small tape recorder to capture the sessions. For weeks after he got back from such trips, Zinnia's father would braise hog meat and play the scratchy tapes for Zinnia and her sister and her mother. Zinnia loved the music, but what she really loved was the crack of the fire, the vultures moaning in the night, the mud-caked men's filthy jokes, the sense of listening to the world's first sounds.

The hunters eventually rid the Wilson ranch of feral hogs, but all they really accomplished was chase them onto adjoining properties. Those owners then leaned on the county to expand its removal program, and Zinnia's father found himself chasing and shooting pigs for decades, with breaks for tours or recording sessions.

Zinnia's mother, meanwhile, held down the house and worked answering the phones at the county call center. From a very early age, Zinnia knew her mother's workplace was a deathly place. When school got out early, she'd take the bus to her mother's office, where her mother sat in a tan cubicle wearing a headset and squeezing a small rubber ball while talking to angry taxpayers. Zinnia would sit on the floor in a corner of her mother's cubicle playing Mega Man on her Game Boy. Even today, she could imitate with precision the deep sighs that issued from her mother when the phone rang—huge gulping sounds that signaled the weary sadness of shift after shift after shift. Whenever Zinnia asked her mother how work was going, the answer was always, "OK." No better, no worse. "OK." Always just, "OK."

Zinnia's sister was named Janet. She was four years older and paid little attention to her. After school, she brought friends back home and locked her bedroom door so Zinnia couldn't bother them. Zinnia lay on the floor of the hallway, listening through the crack at the bottom of the door. Janet and her friends played CDs and laughed, blowing cigarette smoke out the window so Zinnia's parents wouldn't notice the smell. Janet only emerged around dinnertime. She stuck around for their father's nightly music lesson then returned to her room, clicking the lock. She graduated from high school the year before Zinnia started and then moved in with her boyfriend, an auto mechanic who lived on a raggedy boat out in the gulf.

With her father away on hunts, her mother at work, her sister indifferent, Zinnia had no reason not to start selling marijuana. A friend of a friend put her in touch with his brother, who sold at the local community college. Zinnia stored it in a shoe box she kept in a backyard shed her parents never used. She played in her high school jazz band and started selling there; the kids all thought they were beatniks. Soon enough, she was wrapping up bundles of cash in Ziploc bags and storing those, too, out in the shed. Her one splurge: a Technics turntable she used to spin selections from her father's enormous vinyl collection. Her father never once asked where she'd gotten the money to pay for it. The sound of Art Pepper coming off the machine was so crisp he swallowed any questions.

School was hell—populated by dimwits who thought they had a chance in life and rich kids who knew they'd never fail no matter how badly they fucked up. Zinnia dated some, but found every boy she met boring.

Cicely interrupted her. "Wait, wait," she said. She sneezed a glob of green-yellow goop into the sleeve of her shirt. "Wait. So you never had a real boyfriend? Someone you cared about?" Cicely shook her head and blew her nose. "I don't believe that."

Zinnia was sitting next to Cicely's bed with her hands locked around her shins. She tried to look puzzled: "Why's that so hard to believe?"

Cicely tilted her head.

"I mean, did I care for some of the guys? Of course. Some. But are you talking about love? Love?"

"Whatever that means when you're sixteen."

Zinnia unclasped her hands from around her legs and lay back on the floor. With long, calloused fingers, she scratched at the back of her skull. "Maybe not love..."

Senior year. The guy was a park ranger. Jeremy. He had gotten the job straight out of college even though he didn't care at all about saving alligators or scrub jays. He just never wanted to sit in an office.

Zinnia met him at a party a friend from jazz band invited her to. Zinnia's friend and some other kids lit a fire in a quiet spot in the park a couple miles from the main road. Building a fire out there was forbidden, but they figured no one would notice. When Jeremy rolled up on his ATV in his brown uniform, half the party ran for cover, tossing sudsy Solo cups into the grass. Jeremy just laughed and asked if anyone had weed. Of course, Zinnia did, and she shared.

The kids who ran eventually wandered back to the fire— about a dozen or so of them, sitting and lying next to the flames, the hunks of pine popping and hissing and a funnel of smoke circling around them. Jeremy said little that night, but he stayed close to Zinnia, leaning on his elbows and turning slightly her way. He was doughy in the middle and for God's sake he'd have to get rid of that wispy mustache, but Zinnia liked how he looked. His face appeared delighted, even when Zinnia's friends kept going on and on about regionals. By two a.m., the fire had collapsed into hot glowing cubes and Zinnia was cuddling up to Jeremy, leaning over him and kissing him and letting her hair run along the side of his face. Without touching his pants, she knew her lips and tongue were giving him an erection, but she didn't want to do anything but kiss. He gave her a ride back to the main road on his ATV.

She pecked him on the lips saying goodbye. "Shave that fucking mustache," she said. "You look like a retard."

The next weekend, Jeremy brought her to an out-of-the-way spot along the shore of the lake that sat in the center of the park. He waded out into the brown water, shuffling his feet, and called out to Zinnia to follow him. She was nervous—her father always told her to never go swimming in Florida lakes and rivers—but she kicked away her sandals anyway and wandered over to where Jeremy stood, shin-deep. The water was cool and calm. The muck at the bottom of the lake sucked down on her toes. She didn't see any alligators, but she knew they were out there; dark water rippled all around her. It was springtime, and the trees that dangled above the shoreline overflowed with tiny clusters of golden pollen. Zinnia already liked this guy more than most. When he spoke about college, he didn't talk about football or basketball, and instead of bringing her to the new mall like every other guy had, he had taken her here. Also, he had shaved his mustache. Zinnia's feet slurped as she smucked through the mud closer to him. She wrapped her arms around his torso and squeezed.

They dated for three months before Jeremy got shot. Over the years, RVs had begun overrunning the park every spring and summer. The drivers were mostly bored retirees from up north. Since most of them couldn't afford to just rent a place in town, they booked cheap campsites for months at a time and left their enormous metal boxes parked there day and night. Power cables supplied everything they needed—hot water, satellite television, AC—and so they never set foot outside, never took hikes, never toasted marshmallows. They received mail at their campsites and put up cutesy signs decorated with plastic pineapples and teddy bears and flamingos. Around five, they emerged from their RVs and got into cars to drive into town to eat at buffets.

Being the new guy, Jeremy was assigned overnight duty, which meant he had to sleep in the ranger's office at the park's southern entrance and handle any disturbances or complaints. Campers called all night, terrified by suspicious sounds that almost always turned out to be raccoons or possums rooting through trash. That summer, when it grew dark, Zinnia often snuck out of her house and drove her mom's car out to the park, where she and Jeremy would fuck on a cot he set up in the corner of his office.

The call came in one June night while Zinnia was there. Jeremy, his shirt unbuttoned, his belt undone, stuffed a chip in his mouth and answered the landline behind the desk: "What." Zinnia was used to interruptions. She just rolled over and thumbed through an old tabloid. "OK, OK," Jeremy said into the phone. "OK. I'll be there in a minute." He hung up and began buttoning his shirt. "Some fucking RV dude over on loop two is playing a movie too loud and keeping everyone up," Jeremy said.

Zinnia knew it wasn't his fault, but she blamed him for having to leave anyway. "Whatever," she said, not even looking up from her magazine.

"I hate it, too, but what am I... You know what? Never mind. I'll be back."

Zinnia heard him cinch his belt, zip his zipper, and stomp over to the door.

"I didn't look up," Zinnia said. She pulled on her right earlobe. "I should have looked up." She rubbed the back of her neck. "I heard the door slam and the deadbolt. He always locked the door even if I was still there. Then, like, ten minutes later, I heard gunshots."

Cicely was sitting up, her legs crossed, listening intently.

"This old guy shot him. Just unloaded on him through the door of his RV. What I heard was that Jeremy found the RV with the loud movie and it really was blaring, like as loud as a movie theater. People in the RVs around him could hear every single word. So Jeremy starts pounding on the door, yelling at the guy inside."

Zinnia sat up. Her face came level with the bed. Cicely tucked her feet, black with grime, underneath her sheet so Zinnia didn't have to look at them.

"And the guy just started shooting. The news said he told the cops he thought Jeremy was with the ATF. Jeremy was in the hospital and then rehab for a few months, recovering. One of the bullets hit him in the shoulder, which messed up his right arm. The news said another one hit him in the intestines and he got a really bad infection."

Cicely's nose had clogged up. "The news?" she asked, the words deep and deranged. She rubbed drippy snot from the tip of her nose.

"I never went to go see him," Zinnia said. "When I heard the gunshots, I didn't think anything of it at first. Out there, every now and then, you'd hear shots from some of the surrounding ranches, people out hunting. But then I heard the sirens and saw the flashing lights coming and the ambulance going past the ranger's station, and I got freaked out. I wasn't supposed to be there. So I threw on my clothes and drove home. And I just… I just never went to go see him. I saw everything about the shooting, everything about the guy who did it getting off, on the news." Zinnia's head hung down now. "Later on, after he must have been feeling better, he started calling me on my cell phone. But I wouldn't answer. I'd never answer."

Cicely grimaced. What a horrible thing to admit. But senior year. Zinnia was, what, seventeen. Eighteen. Cicely leaned over and put her arm on Zinnia's shoulder, but Zinnia brushed her off, stood up, and walked into her own bedroom. Her door crashed shut.

A clear-skinned anole scampered up the orange wall opposite Cicely's bed. A few feet from the ceiling, it paused, turned its head, and glanced around the room. The lizard's dewlap puffed in and out, in and out, in and out. When the anole's eyes met Cicely's, she threw a pillow at it. She missed, but the lizard dropped to the floor. It crawled into a narrow crack in the baseboard and disappeared.

27.

After Cicely's sixth run, Zinnia told her she'd introduce her to their client, the doula, who called herself Anna. The next morning, a Thursday, Cicely and Zinnia walked together to the tower and retrieved the cold bag of placentas.

Anna lived on the opposite side of the bridge, on one of the barrier islands that paralleled the coast. It was late, already almost ten o'clock, but the whole town seemed to just be waking up. A mist that had settled over the bay was slowly evaporating as the day grew hotter. The sun climbed up Cicely's and Zinnia's backs as they walked westward; their shadows grew shorter and shorter. Once on the island, they scampered across the road and hopped over a low wooden fence and carefully scooted down a steep sandy incline. They followed a trail that ran along the edge of the island.

"Here we are," Zinnia whispered, pointing to what looked to Cicely like nothing but a tangled mass of mangroves and vines. But Zinnia ducked into a small opening in the wall of green and disappeared. Cicely clutched the cold and perspiring plastic bag filled with placentas to her chest and followed her friend. After duck-walking a few steps, she was able to stand up straight again, as the narrow trail widened into a clearing in the middle of which stood a trailer. The gray sand glade was shrouded in greenery except for a broad circle directly above the trailer, whose reflective aluminum roof gleamed amid a shower of sunshine. A propane tank sat next to the trailer. A red rubber hose grew from its nozzle and disappeared into the trailer's recesses. A stout wooden post held up a green water faucet nearby. A thick cable of some kind ran from the trees and into a window; it had been duct-taped to the side of the trailer to keep it from flailing in the wind. A pile of logs acted as steps up to the trailer's rounded door. "Here we are," Zinnia repeated. She looked nervous; she kept rubbing her hands against her thighs. She knocked.

Someone pushed aside the floral curtain in the door's small window and then the door clicked open an inch or two. Zinnia reached up and pulled it open all the way. Anna wasn't visible through the darkness inside, but Cicely followed Zinnia into the trailer. Holding the placentas with one hand, Cicely closed the door behind her. The space inside seemed so much bigger than it did from outside. A kitchenette was set into one end of the trailer; bunk beds stood on the opposite side. A laptop sat on the lower mattress. The screen showed a rainy streetscape cut through with headlights. In the open middle of the room sat a furry orange couch, a glass coffee table, and an assortment of oddities: a bulging, waist-tall drum, shelves lined with small figurines, a stack of cookbooks big enough to serve as a chair. Flowery fabrics hung along the walls and from the ceiling. A curlicue-patterned rug stretched over most of the floor. Cicely would have described the vibe as trailer park opium den.

Anna herself was short and fat, draped in drooping fabrics. She hugged Zinnia tightly and did the same to Cicely.

"Let me turn this off," Anna said, walking back toward the beds. After hitting pause on the laptop, Anna held an ivory pipe to her lips and puffed. The air smelled tangy from whatever she was smoking. Not tobacco, not marijuana—Cicely couldn't place the scent.

"You're just in time for breakfast," Anna said, clapping her hands together. Her voice was high and squeaky. Anna walked to Cicely and held out her hands.

It took Cicely a moment to realize she wanted the placentas. "Oh, sorry," Cicely said, handing over the bag. Was that the breakfast Anna was talking about? Thinking about the metallic blood scent of the placentas nauseated Cicely all over again. "I'm not hungry," Cicely said, meekly, "but thank you."

Anna shook her head as she placed the bag in her refrigerator. "Nope, nope. I insist. How can we do business together if we haven't shared a meal." Anna's back was turned to them. Cicely looked at Zinnia and raised her eyebrows, but Zinnia just shrugged.

"Has Lisa's stuff been OK?" Zinnia asked Anna. Cicely guessed Lisa was the nurse at the hospital who dropped the bags to her.

"So far, so good," Anna said, clanging around in a cabinet and coming up with a wide Teflon-coated pan. She set the pan on her short white stove and turned the knob to fire up the burner. On the white plastic cutting board to her right lay a purplish lump of something soft and slick. With a long silver blade, Anna began cutting into the tissue, slicing out thin strips from the stringy clump of offal. Once that was done, she dusted the slices with rotund crystals of salt and poured oil into the now-hot pan. The fat filled the trailer's air with a grassy fragrance. Cicely couldn't believe it, but the gentle pain of hunger began to spread through her belly.

Zinnia sat down on the couch and pulled an Indian cookbook from the massive pile. She leafed through it, concentrating on the photos. Cicely tried to catch her attention, but Zinnia ignored her. Cicely didn't want to let her down, didn't want to embarrass her in front of Anna, didn't want to cost her money, didn't want to admit out loud she was nervous, didn't want to do anything that might jeopardize the peace she had made with life in the past few weeks. She had imagined that meeting Anna, taking on a bigger role in her operation, might free her from the hall, from having to walk around with her breasts showing, serving Cub Scouts and degenerates, but here she was, about to be force-fed a part of a human body and too intimidated to even open her mouth.

The meat hissed as Anna laid it delicately in the pan. The iron scent of the searing placenta drifted from the kitchenette.

Anna set a small white timer for four minutes. "Can't move

it at all," she said, turning around to face Cicely. "The key is to just let it sit there and caramelize on one side."

Cicely just nodded. Her face was hot and suddenly wet. She hadn't eaten anything for breakfast and her stomach both hurt from hunger and churned with anxiety. The smell wafting through the air wasn't as disgusting as she would have guessed.

Whistling, Anna walked to Cicely and put her hands on Cicely's upper arms. "Tell me about yourself, Cicely," she said. What? What did that even mean? "Do you have any children?"

Cicely shook her head.

"Me neither," Anna said. She clasped her hands together and looked down. "My eggs are all cracked up."

Zinnia tossed the cookbook she was looking at back on the pile. The smack of it landing made Cicely jump. Zinnia just picked up another book and continued browsing.

"I don't even know if mine are all right, really," Cicely said. She had never before thought she might be infertile. She had risked sex without a condom a few times, knew it was stupid, but had never considered the possibility she couldn't have a kid. It would be delicious relief to know she couldn't bring someone else into this world.

"You're young," Anna said. "You never know until you try." The pan went quiet and a sliver of smoke puffed into the air. Right as Anna twirled back to pull out the meat, the timer went off. "Perfect!" She scooped the blackened knob from the pan and set it on a white oval plate, then added another morsel to the pan. The green oil popped angrily.

Cicely tapped the taut skin of the drum that stood in a corner near the couch. She kept looking to Zinnia, hoping she would intervene, would at least say something, but Zinnia wasn't paying attention. Cicely smacked the drum loudly. Zinnia still didn't look up, but Anna heard and she walked over. She rhythmically rubbed the drum's dry, scratchy surface then slapped it gently on and off.

Anna's head drifted back and forth. She closed her eyes. "Kind of hard to believe this is real skin, isn't it?"

Cicely jerked her hands away and took a step back. Anna cackled. Was she joking? Just playing on Cicely's nerves?

"Kind of fucked up, huh? But someone like you, someone who used to work for me, made this." Anna kept the rhythm going with her fingertips. "She worked at a hospital out east and once she started stealing placentas she started walking out with all kinds of weird shit." Anna's high-pitched voice was annoying before—now it sounded menacing, like that of a malevolent toddler. Anna straightened her head and opened her eyes and pointed to the figurines lined up on the shelf near the bunk beds. "From bones, mostly. Her boyfriend knew how to carve." She took down a brown tea cozy that hung from a nail beaten into an exposed two-by-four and handed it to Cicely, who rubbed its rope-like fabric. "Hair," Anna said.

Cicely tried to hand the cozy back to her, but Anna scampered over to the kitchenette. The pan had gone quiet again and the second lump was ready. Zinnia set the cookbook back on the pile. Cicely whipped the tea cozy at her. Pulling it open, Zinnia set it on her head. Hair on hair—the thought made Cicely laugh and eased some of the tension she felt. Zinnia had taken care of her, hadn't she? Why worry as long as she was around? Cicely made up her mind: if Anna offered her placenta, and if Zinnia ate it, she'd eat it, too, hold her nose and force it down, maybe, but eat it. According to Zinnia, Anna's clients reported that eating placenta helped them sleep more deeply, leached toxins from their bones, and even cleared up acne and made their breath smell better. Maybe, Cicely thought, it could work miracles.

The timer rang again. Anna pulled three rolls from a small toaster oven on the counter then poured hot water into three immense mugs. From the cabinet below the sink she pulled a big jar that was half-filled with loose clumps of tea. She brought everything over to the glass coffee table, including the plate with the three nibbles of meat, which were caramelized almost to black on one side. Over the placenta Anna had drizzled fragrant oil and sticky strands of honey; she had then dusted the plate with toasted cumin seeds. No, it didn't smell good, no, not that, but it smelled better than when Cicely had opened the bag and sniffed the placentas raw.

Zinnia scooped tea leaves into her mug and snatched a roll while Anna brought over forks and knives and napkins. Cicely only vaguely remembered the last time someone had invited her into a home and prepared an actual meal for her. It was a guy named Jude she knew from back when she worked at the Ponderosa, a fellow server who fancied himself a chef. But his oven went haywire and his lasagna burned up so badly the top was ashy, so instead he ordered pizza and they got drunk on red wine and watched a movie from the seventies, which she remembered only because all the men in the movie wore mutton chops.

"To our new partnership," Anna said, raising her mug. She settled down onto the rug next to the coffee table. With her flowing clothes, she looked like a little mound of person there on the floor.

"Do we really have to eat this shit?" Zinnia asked, her mouth full of roll.

Anna's expression turned hard. "Everyone." She cut herself a small nugget and popped it into her mouth. Cicely was sitting on her knees, her butt resting on her heels. She watched Anna chew. Anna suddenly stood. "I'll show you." She walked over to a cork board that hung on the back of the door and pulled down a Polaroid. Shoving it in Zinnia's face, she snarled. "This is what ended up happening the last time I let someone say no."

Zinnia's expression dropped and her face went pale; she handed the photo to Cicely. It showed the face of a young woman, her eyes closed, her head twisted at an odd angle, her hair glued to her forehead with sweat and grime. It was hard to tell, but it looked like the back of her head was resting on scratchy gray concrete. Snot trickled out of her nose and tiny pinpricks of blood dotted her cheeks and forehead, as if someone, Anna, apparently, had taken a tiny needle and repeatedly jabbed it into her skin. Cicely had just begun feeling comfortable in this trailer. The photo reminded her that she was involved in a criminal enterprise, and that she was in no way safe.

"If you're in, you're in," Anna said, snatching back the photo. As she put it back on the cork board, Zinnia and Cicely exchanged stunned glances. Cicely thought Zinnia could protect her; this moment told her she was wrong.

With a wry grin, Zinnia cut herself a knotted chunk of placenta. Cicely did the same.

Anna hit play on a stereo hidden behind some drapes. The dulcet synthesizers of a New Age track radiated gently from the speakers. As late morning shifted toward noon, and the sun reached its zenith, the rays filtering through the windows slowly died out and the light inside the air seemed to soften. Anna rejoined Cicely and Zinnia by the coffee table. She stared intently at Cicely, who was staring intently at the black, gray, purple, red chunk of human at the tip of her fork. Cicely heard Zinnia begin chewing. Breathing deeply through her nose, her heart pulsating wildly, her stomach sending up desperate signals of no, Cicely crunched her eyes shut and took a bite.

28.

One night after work, Cicely took the wrong bus, the one that went downtown, west, toward her old home, and when she saw the arc of the empty bridge she had crossed so many times on foot, carrying dinner, the air whistling around her, she thought of him.

Nostalgia surprised her, her thoughts skipping past misery, theft, and cruelty, and settling on sensations from long-ago Tuesday mornings when they would get ready to go to the St. Mark's services. Not having to go to the hall later always put Cicely in a pleasant mood. Cicely knew she was kidding herself, living inside her head, as she often did during those years, daydreaming that this or that little thing she did for her father would make him love her, make him shake off his rage and hatred, make her visible to him. As if, during the hundredth time she tied his tie, he would snap out of himself, feel the care she gave him, and realize how awful he had been. It never happened. But when he wasn't around, it was easy for Cicely to fantasize that it would. Next time, next time. He'll come around. She always felt alone, so alone. Neighbors looked the other way when she joined them at the bus stop. Deep inside, Cicely knew that nothing she did, nothing she thought, nothing she expressed, mattered.

Cicely's nostalgia burned away and her mind returned to the night she handed over her father to the Owner and his golf course. Whole weeks had passed during which she never once wondered what had become of her father. She felt no guilt. She didn't care in the least what the Owner or the man with the box cutter was making him do. The image of her father chopping vines and spraying poisonous orange chemicals next to ex-convicts and drug addicts and deadbeats filled her with elation. If only she could see it, could watch him be humiliated.

Would he come home after he served his time? Cicely wondered what he would think when he found the house empty, when he realized he was all alone. He would wander around the abandoned rooms, see that all her things were gone, plop down on the tarp, and bawl.

If she felt bad about any of it, it was shame that she didn't feel bad, shock at how easy it was to sever herself from him. She wished the Owner had kidnapped him sooner.

29.

She spent ten bucks on a used Discman at Goodwill and another ten on a set of furry headphones and a cord that connected the CD player to the tape deck in Zinnia's van. From the library she checked out a handful of CDs, all ones she had loved in high school.

Zinnia told her she was way out of date. Nobody cared about just one person sitting on a stool with an acoustic guitar anymore, she said. But that's how Zinnia's music sounded to Cicely. Zinnia used a band, but when they performed, every note seemed to come from Zinnia, as if Zinnia, in that dress that still sparkled even though Cicely had never seen her wash it, was transmitting the music from somewhere else, as if she was an antenna vibrating with music from another place. And you could feel the roots in what Zinnia sang. The synthesizers needed to be plugged in, the bass was electric, but Cicely could hear the old mountain songs through all that, the murder ballads and bootlegging tales.

They were eating empanadas and drinking gin laced with Sprite one night when Zinnia asked Cicely if she wanted to hear a new song. This was a first. Cicely didn't know when or where Zinnia wrote her tunes, if they came spontaneously during rehearsal or if she deliberately sat down to write.

"Of course I'd like to hear," Cicely said, surprised at how overwhelmed she felt.

While Zinnia rummaged in Cicely's room for the right instrument, Cicely sliced an empanada in half. Cheese oozed out. Zinnia emerged with a long plastic keyboard, but banging on the keys released no sound. "Must need batteries. Hold on." Cicely could hear her rifling through boxes in her bedroom. In the meantime, she bit into the empanada and took a slug of gin.

Zinnia reappeared and dumped the keyboard's old batteries out onto the floor.

"When did you write it?" Cicely asked.

"The other day."

More gin. "Where? I never see you practicing."

The new batteries clicked into place. "Usually after rehearsals, I stick around for an hour in the shed and try to come up with some stuff." Zinnia snapped the plastic back over the batteries. "Or just work on stuff I've already written." Zinnia pressed a few keys. The sound was tinny.

Cicely drank again. Her head was beginning to feel warm. She had to concentrate on enunciating: "I can't wait."

With the keyboard in her lap, Zinnia sat in a low beach chair. Cicely was on the floor, the paper plate with the empanada balanced on her crossed legs. Even in her worn-out gray sweats, even with her white hair pulled back below a headband, even as she picked her nose, Zinnia looked radiant. She pressed out a few chords and then took a deep breath.

Even though Cicely had witnessed the transformation many times at work, the way Zinnia's voice shifted when she sang still amazed her. Zinnia's speaking voice—so low, kind of ugly— disappeared, warping into this soft dreamlike haze.

Zinnia's song began with a series of shimmering, droning chords, then a slow progression up and down the keyboard. She sang about dead lovers, about bodies in bags being dragged to shorelines, about men falling out of planes, about fingers found in the belly of an alligator. There was no chorus, but the verses always circled back and ended on one common phrase: "He took my heart," Zinnia sang, the last syllable extending into a long vibrato. "I took him." The tune ended with a low, desperate moan that stretched on and on, even after Zinnia had stopped playing the keys.

Cicely was sure the song would sound good fleshed out by

Zinnia's band, but it wouldn't sound better. The weak notes from the keyboard only made the growl at the heart of the song that much scarier. Listening to it was like watching Zinnia strip off her clothes item by item then slowly scrape off her skin, too.

"Beautiful," Cicely said. When she lunged up at Zinnia for a hug, her elbow knocked over her gin. A puddle of booze and soda spread on the floor. Cicely stopped halfway into the hug. "Oh shit," she said, jumping up to get a towel from the kitchen.

"Bring back the bottle," Zinnia said. "You'll need a refill." She glugged her drink. "Me, too, in fact."

The booze, the song, her closeness to Zinnia—everything conspired to deliver a jolt of happiness.

After soaking up the spill, Cicely poured more alcohol for both of them, leaving an inch at the top for soda. Cicely sat back on the floor. "Where do your songs come from?"

"Dreams, fantasies." Zinnia shrugged. "Other songs."

Dreams and fantasies—Cicely had those, but they usually hurt. Every reminder of what her life wasn't, what her life didn't have, stung. She felt so old, just twenty-five but with nothing at all, no destination, nothing to excite her. The next day meant waking up and going to work, the day after that meant waking up and going to work, the day after that the same, the whole continuum just a stretch of hours that were filled with—what?—with nothing, just do this, do this, do this. In another twenty-five years she'd be fifty and in another twenty-five she'd be seventy-five, and then what. Then she'd die at some point, and for what. Just to die, to end the story. She was born, so she had to die. In between were just days, days that were born in the east and that died in the west, with the sun collapsing into a gulf choked with dead fish and dolphins and birds.

Cicely turned her head away. She ran her hand on the floor where she had spilled her drink. It still felt tacky. Sugar ants would be all over the spot by morning.

"You all right?" Zinnia asked.

Surely everyone thinks this way at some point, Cicely told herself. Everyone knows how pointless it all is. So why does everyone seem so OK with it? Happy to just sit there and let it happen. Or maybe these thoughts never cross their mind.

Cicely felt Zinnia's fingers on her shoulder. Cicely pushed her hand away. She didn't want sympathy.

Cicely's mind fixed on an idea. She did some quick math, tried to remember today's date. Wiping her face, she turned back to Zinnia. "Do you think your van could make it to Orlando?"

30.

The government stopped home mail delivery shortly after the crash, so Cicely couldn't send out anything till her next shift at work. She stole an envelope, a sheet of paper, a pen, and a stamp from the manager's office and sat at the bar writing out her note:

> M.,
>   I'm coming for you. I'm not sure when, but
> I am.
>   C.

Her handwriting was bad, out of practice. It slanted to the right, but not evenly. It looked like a middle schooler's script. The final C was ragged and irregular. Her father's neck. On the envelope, she scrawled the PO number she had memorized and the rest of the address. She handed it to Dwayne and asked him to send it.

"Finally writing back to your dreamboat?" he asked. He had lightened in his attitude toward her lately, as if their common criminality somehow bonded them. Two months ago, the joke would have pissed her off—now she just smiled.

"Telling him about this guy Dwayne I know with a dick the size of a clothespin."

"Ha." Dwayne slapped the envelope between his palms and carried it to the outgoing mail slot in the back. Cicely had begun trusting him, but she watched him the whole way. The envelope dropped from Dwayne's hand into the slit.

Tonight's booking was a shell show. Cicely couldn't imagine anything more boring. The men and women hauled in plastic tubs loaded with shells wrapped in protective paper towels and set out their displays on card tables arranged in long rows throughout the hall. Few vendors showed up. Cicely guessed that the dead fish prevented enthusiasts from scouring the beaches. The offerings were minor.

Delivering waters and coffees, Cicely saw chipped oyster shells, scallop shells encrusted with small stones, mussel shells that had lost their luster. She loved handling big fluted conch shells, but there were none of those tonight. The vendors seemed depressed. With few customers to sell to, they gathered in small circles and gossiped about the dead fish.

Cicely spent most of the night hanging back and watching Dwayne. She didn't know exactly how he sold his pills, couldn't tell where he kept his stash. If she was making as much as she was carting placentas, she could only imagine how much he was earning. And if she could get her hands on his supply? But who could she sell them to? Zinnia had already told her pills were out of their league, and Cicely knew no one else. Still.

Cicely's attention snapped to when she heard an old woman mention the Owner. The lady wore a red leather vest over a pink blouse, with jacaranda-print trousers. Cicely edged closer to the conversation.

The old woman's jowls vibrated as she spoke: "… how this town works. Whatever you want, just buy it."

"But has the runoff even been tested?" asked one of the men she was addressing.

"Does it need to be?" the woman retorted. "You know what they use. You're old enough to remember that course they tried to build in the nineties, right on the gulf. Remember the junk they were pumping out?" The men around nodded glumly.

"All right!" a man across the room shouted. "Show's over!"

The circle around the old woman broke up and the men went back to their tables and started packing up their unsold merchandise. The old woman turned to her table and began rewrapping her shells in paper towels. Delanna and Hilda had already begun clearing dirty glasses from the tables. Cicely knew she needed to help them, but she walked up to the old woman instead and gently tapped her on the back, as if she were afraid she might bruise her. The old woman turned around.

"Ma'am, I couldn't help but overhear…" Cicely fidgeted. "You mentioned the golf course being built. By the Owner? Some runoff?"

The old woman smoothed out the fabric of her vest. She looked annoyed. "Miss, I find it difficult to take you seriously with your bosoms hanging out." She went back to her shells and spoke to Cicely only over her shoulder: "Lord knows what your parents must think."

"Nobody makes you come here."

The old woman's shoulders sagged. "Go away please."

Driving home, the van slammed into a small flock of white ibises. Zinnia hit the brakes and Cicely hopped out to survey the damage. Blood and feathers were scattered all over the road. Thin, pink legs lay sprawled across the blacktop. One bird was still hopping, over by the edge of the road, where it graveled up before slipping down into a small gutter. One of its legs had been knocked off around the knee; all that was left was a gory stump. The bird was trying to make its way off the road, into the swarm of palms that blanketed the edge of the street, but it kept tipping over, its narrow beak throwing out weak screams. Red dots of blood stippled its white feathers. Cicely took a step toward the bird, but it turned its head and shrieked, freezing her. Her sandals stuck to the road, the blood a soft glue between her sole and the ground.

The one-legged ibis hopped down into the gutter and up into the strand of palms, where it collapsed, wings flapping. Cicely climbed into the van. Zinnia gunned the engine. Behind them, they left two long streaks of bloody tire tracks.

31.

One-fifteen and the nurse in the pink scrubs still hadn't showed. Cicely paced along the sidewalk, looking up into the dark recesses of the hospital's footbridge.

The thought of letting down Anna terrified Cicely. She kept thinking of the face of the girl in the photo, the one with the puncture wounds all over it, wondering what she looked like after the bleeding stopped. It was a still, quiet night—the hospital seemed deserted—but Cicely's ears roared with panic.

As her sandals scuffed back and forth along the rough pavement, she reverted to an old bad habit: chewing her nails. In middle school, she'd often bite down on her nails till her fingers stung. She also picked at her cuticles, tearing off the small flaps of skin that curved up around the edges of her nails. Blood would slip out and run along the rim of the nail, lining it with dark maroon. She'd suck on her fingers and then press them frantically to her clothes, trying to stop the flow. At some point, she lost the habit, but in times of stress it returned.

She took another look up. The bridge hung there, empty and dark. Its left side connected to the second story of a three-story parking garage, also silent and black at this hour. The hospital had built a little guard hut at the entrance to the garage, but with so few people able to afford cars, it made no sense to staff it, and so it too sat empty, the yellow and black striped rail that once blocked the driveway now just stuck permanently in the up position.

Cicely started the van and checked the clock: one-twenty.

She leaned back and again looked up at the bridge. She thought about Anna, about the taste of the placenta, about the money she'd miss, about what Zinnia's face would look like when she found out Cicely didn't have the delivery—all a blur—and then she backed up and pulled into the parking garage.

The low concrete ceiling and the tight walls made the groan of the van's engine reverberate even more loudly than usual. The headlights swung around the corner at the top of the first ramp, revealing more gray cement and red signs with doctors' names on them. Tapping the brake pedal, Cicely inched the van up to the doorway that opened out onto the bridge. She could see through to the other side now, the hospital side, where bright fluorescent lights shone through a wide sliding glass door.

Cicely left the van running and tiptoed out onto the bridge. There was no sign of anyone, anything, no bag left for her, no note. Through the door on the far side, she could see a long, cream-colored hallway, decorated with photos of men and women in white lab coats. Farther down the hall, she saw a desk with a few nurses and doctors clustered around, talking. Confident they couldn't see her because of the reflection on their side of the glass, Cicely walked out farther onto the bridge, out to where the nurse usually stood. She leaned over and glanced down to where she normally caught the placentas, her eyes struck by a ghostly image of herself still pacing down there, still biting her nails.

Stepping back, she turned to the glowing hospital door. The nurses and doctors had concluded their discussion at the end of the hallway, but a pair of doctors—both gray-haired, one male, one female—lingered. Had their presence prevented the pink-haired nurse from making the drop? Or had she been caught? The idea startled Cicely. If the nurse with the pink hair had been caught, she would surely turn on Cicely, and she knew Zinnia's van, so she, too, was implicated.

When Cicely took a step toward the glass doors, they whooshed open. She jumped back, startled. She remained several yards away from the doors—why had they opened? Down the hall, the two doctors both looked in her direction, and in that moment she saw herself through their eyes, standing out on the dark bridge, dressed in sandals with black worn-down soles and jeans with threads beginning to show around the knees, sucking on her fingers, her tank top dotted with small smudges of blood, acne bumping along the edges of her face, no makeup, her total lack of bag or purse marking her as a stranger, maybe even a hobo, maybe even someone violent and crazed, her expression one of fear and surprise, looking like a raccoon trapped in a flashlight, her face gone blank, and now she was scurrying, yes, scurrying away, bolting from the open glass doors and back across the bridge to the van.

By the time the van swung around the garage toward the ramp that led downstairs, the two gray-haired doctors, befuddled, had stepped through the sliding glass doors. The van's tires squealed as the machine rounded the corner and down onto the ramp. It jerked up and down as Cicely gassed it out onto the street. She had no placentas and no explanation and she'd been seen.

32.

Zinnia didn't seem concerned when Cicely told her what happened. She just said she'd pass along word to Anna. Still, Cicely had trouble sleeping the next couple nights. She often couldn't tell if she was dreaming or awake, springing up in bed, thinking Anna was there, in the room, or that she was outside, circling the house, or that the cops were shining flashlights through the windows. But Zinnia seemed calm, so Cicely held everything inside, just told Zinnia she was tired when Zinnia asked why she wasn't talking much. The worry in her stomach eased while she was at work, when she was forced to concentrate on something else, but as soon as she was alone again, it returned.

What was she even doing this for? She had become fixated on the idea of visiting her mother, but why? To spite her? To curse her? To embrace her? To be taken care of? Cicely didn't know what she expected to happen when she did make it to Orlando, let alone what she expected after coming back from Orlando. The placenta thing couldn't last. Cicely saw that now.

On Saturday afternoon, Anna summoned both of them to her trailer. She hugged them as they entered. Cicely expected her to be furious, but her greeting contained no hostility. She stroked Cicely's hair and kissed her on the cheek.

The same New Age music she played last time was issuing from the stereo. The song sounded like small twinkling bells intertwined with whale moans. Zinnia wrinkled her nose at the sound: "How can you listen to this stuff?"

Anna giggled. "It keeps me calm." She wore billowing linen

pants and a silky blue top beneath an apron that read Kill the Cook. Something was sizzling in the trailer's small oven, leaving the air smoky and greasy. It didn't smell like placenta, but Cicely's stomach still quivered. "I was just going to open the windows," Anna said, noticing how Cicely recoiled from the smell.

Anna walked over to the small glass panes that lined the far side of the trailer and popped them open. The windows had no screens. As Anna opened them, a few mosquitoes drifted in and began circling the women. "Stand perfectly still," Anna said, watching as one of the bugs landed on the knuckles of Cicely's right hand. Anna pulled a large wooden spoon from the pocket of her apron and before Cicely could protest she rapped her hard across the hand. The sting made Cicely shout. Anna looked for blood on the spoon. "Damn," she said. "Missed."

Cicely rubbed her hands together. Zinnia laughed.

"Have a seat," Anna said.

Opening the windows dispersed the grease from the air, but now the heat and humidity crept in. Anna's small AC unit couldn't keep up. The room felt fuzzy—the purpose of this meeting suddenly less real. Cicely wanted to giggle but didn't. "Let's get to it," she said.

Cicely's directness surprised Zinnia, who raised her eyebrows.

"Fine," Anna said, untying her apron. She hung it from a nail stuck in the wall and grabbed her pipe. "Bottom line: the doctors figured out what was what."

"Oof," Zinnia said. "That sucks."

Anna nodded as she lit the bowl of the pipe and sucked in smoke. Again, it wasn't tobacco, and it wasn't marijuana.

"What are you smoking?" Cicely asked. It surprised her how little she cared about the news from the hospital.

Anna looked surprised, too. "It's a blend one of my mamas makes for me. It's a mix of a bunch of stuff—weeds, tea leaves, herbs. She says it detoxes your lungs, but..." She laughed. "I don't know about that." She handed the pipe to Cicely, who put it to her lips. Anna's saliva still coated the pipe's tip. Cicely inhaled. The smoke tasted strong, way stronger than anything she had smoked before. It scorched her lungs. She coughed. "Yeah, pretty much everybody coughs the first time," Anna said.

"Can we talk about the hospital?" Zinnia asked.

Anna winked at Cicely then took another puff. "They fired Lisa straight away. She came sobbing to me and told me everything. Some new night shift nurse, an Eagle Scout type, walked in on her stuffing placentas into a bag and ratted her out."

"How do you know she didn't rat you out?"

Smoke drifted out of Anna's nostrils. "They don't care. They don't want cops sniffing around. The docs are into way worse shit."

"Pills," Cicely said.

Anna nodded. "And probably worse. Lisa's just making a nurse's salary. What's their excuse?"

Zinnia: "So you're not worried. At all."

Anna shook her head. "No reason to be."

She handed the pipe back to Cicely, who inhaled again and drew the smoke down into her lungs, where it seemed to float. Cicely felt her chest open, her head lighten. She shivered.

"I know, right?" Anna said. She took back the pipe. "I'd offer you some from my stash, but with Lisa fired, I'm out a thousand a week. Austerity."

Cicely and Zinnia, lost in their private worries, didn't speak the whole walk home.

Once inside, Cicely needed to pee. When she went to close the door to the bathroom, she heard Zinnia from the living room: "You don't need to close the door, you know."

Cicely took her hand from the cold door handle and glanced at her reflection in the mirror. Whenever there had been a bathroom door for Cicely to close, she'd always closed it, had never thought twice about it, even when she was home alone. She'd always been self-conscious about the noise she made when she urinated, the splash that sounded so loud to her sitting there on the bowl, always thinking it was louder than anyone else's, as if whoever was on the other side of the door or even on the other side of the house or even outside could hear and was judging her. Her mother had always closed the door—always.

It was funny what she remembered. The depth of shame. The small, stupid gestures.

Leaving the door half-open, she sat on the toilet, the seat surprisingly warm, and began to pee, adjusting her posture so the urine fell on the front of the bowl, not in the water.

She leaned over and rubbed her legs. She barely ever shaved them. Work required her to wear tights, so no one ever saw them, so what was the point. The only part of her body she did shave was her underarms. The manager at the dance hall made it clear that was mandatory.

The prickly hairs on her calves scratched at her palms as she rubbed up and down. Her panties looked so small lying on the ground between her legs. Cicely's last few drops of urine splashed into the puddle in the toilet. She yanked up her underwear and buttoned her jeans. Before flushing, Cicely watched her pale golden bubbles circle the bowl.

33.

It finally rained again. But it wasn't like last time. It didn't come in an unstoppable rush—it snuck up on the city, the sky fading from aquamarine to gray, so incrementally you wouldn't even notice, then little wisps of wind fluttered around, scattering leaves, making you rub your bare arms, then the dense humidity, the first engorged droplets plunking down on cement, metal, tar, then a strange lightening, the drops dissolving into air till the whole sky filled with a soft mist.

The rain lingered, graying the sky for a week and making the dead fish stink worse than it had been in weeks, as if all the moisture, rather than washing away the filth, was instead fermenting the corpses. The whole fishing village, the street Cicely and Zinnia lived on, their backyard, turned acrid.

Traffic on the roads went from slow to nonexistent—no one was going near the beach now—and Cicely, now again dependent on money from the hall to get by, experienced a series of painfully slow nights at work. After they subtracted the cost of her meal at the end of the night, she barely had anything left. Zinnia struggled too, and after two days they were eating the canned food at the back of the kitchen cabinet that the previous tenants had left behind, the gelatinous refried beans and pickled jalapeños and bland salsa of some long-ago taco night.

On the fourth night of the rain, Cicely found the man with the box cutter waiting for her in the parking lot when she left work. She froze. His outfit—his sawed-off boots, his red bandanna—hadn't changed, except tonight he wore a yellow poncho. Cicely couldn't see the box cutter in his belt, but his hand hid under the yellow plastic, and she knew what it was touching.

"The Owner would like to see you," he said, taking his hand, empty, from beneath the poncho. He raised both palms as if he were under arrest.

It wasn't even October yet. Was the Owner reneging on their deal? The idea that something bad might have happened to her father blipped somewhere. "I can't tonight," she said, her voice more unsteady than she had hoped.

The man grinned. A piece of chewed food—something green, spinach?—had caught in one of his gold teeth. He flicked his tongue at her. It looked purple, like a gila monster's. "This is a social call."

Cicely cocked her head to the left. It sounded like bullshit. She remembered the knock of her head hitting the wall when the man now standing in front of her had shoved her. She remembered the blood winding down her arm. She remembered the brown blade against her cheek. "And if I say no?"

Turning his palms upward, he shrugged. "Then he'll be disappointed."

It wasn't a threat—she heard that in his tone. Then what was it? He pulled a keyring from his pocket; the metal tinkled in his hand. The tongue in the dance hall sign flashed on and off, a pulsating red haze in the slow drizzle. Cicely's hair was beginning to stick to her forehead and underneath her chin.

"Well?" the man asked.

"Not tonight."

Exasperated: "Then name a night."

"Night after tomorrow. I'm off."

"Okey-dokey. He'll pick you up at home."

"I don't live there anymore."

The man smirked, as if it were naive of her to think he didn't know that. He climbed up into his truck, the tires as tall as Cicely. When the engine cranked on, so did the radio, and a talk show poured out of the cab at top volume. It was Father Bill speaking, his weekly show, rebroadcast over and over all week long. "God wants you to succeed!" he was insisting, the volume in the truck so high that it distorted his voice and turned the lower frequencies into a brutal buzz.

The man remembered something and killed the radio. "Wear something nice," he shouted down to Cicely—too loudly, as if the radio were still on.

Back home, Cicely asked Zinnia if she could borrow her sparkly dress for the evening.

"Why not just tell this guy to screw off?" Zinnia asked. She was miffed. Cicely couldn't tell if it was about the dress or something else.

Cicely was eating a grilled cheese sandwich from the hall. Orange goo clung to her fingers. "He was nice to me." Another crunchy bite. "It's not like anybody else is asking me to get dressed up."

Zinnia scoffed. "That's pathetic. So any asshole comes along—"

"Come on. Don't be like that."

Zinnia got up off the floor and stalked over to the kitchen window, which looked out over the backyard. There were no streetlights in this part of the village, and all Cicely could see in the window was Zinnia's reflection. She looked like she was thinking about what to say next. But instead of speaking, she simply opened the window and threw out the remnants of her dinner. The rain outside simmered. Zinnia slammed the window shut and dumped her Styrofoam box in the sink, then brushed past Cicely and headed for the bathroom. "Sure you can borrow it," she said, without looking back. "I'm getting ready for bed."

When the day came, Cicely rode the bus downtown to turn in the CDs she had borrowed and to find new ones: *On the Beach*, *New Morning*, more Joni. On the way home, the bus passed the field where St. Mark's was broadcasting Father Bill's sermon. Through the grimy bus window, she could make out the swirling crowd, bigger than she remembered, the red-robed volunteers with their golden trays collecting donations, and the giant screen, which seemed even taller and wider and brighter than she remembered.

Father Bill's face looked even bigger, his yellow teeth the size of window curtains. The screen flashed so sharply in the gray day that it hurt to look at it directly for too long. As the bus idled, Cicely could hear Father Bill's loud voice rolling over the grass of the field. He was speaking on the parable of the talents.

"… cast ye out the unprofitable servant into the outer darkness! 'Unprofitable'! What an ugly word. What an insult. God's judgment…" The bus started rolling again and Cicely lost Father Bill's voice.

Zinnia's dress fit Cicely well enough, but it was tighter than anything she'd worn in years. When she bent over, the fabric cinched around her waist; she couldn't reach lower than her calves. Zinnia, still annoyed, left for work early so she wouldn't be around while Cicely got ready.

Cicely kept looking at her reflection in the mirror that hung on the back of the door in Zinnia's room, turning this way and that. The dress still shimmered like it did when Cicely first saw Zinnia in it. When she adjusted her hips or shook an ankle, the white coins stitched into the fabric rattled. She rubbed her stomach. She hoped the Owner wasn't taking her out for a big meal—she might split open the dress.

After carefully sliding out of it, she shaved her legs. As careful as she was, she still nicked herself around the tendon that stretched behind her right knee. When the Owner's long white car pulled up, she was still sporting the tissue she put on the cut to dry it, the flaky white paper darkened by a bloody red oval.

34.

Aside from the basic compliments, the Owner said little to Cicely during the drive and gave her no indication where they were headed. When they pulled into the parking lot at his building downtown, the same building the man with the box cutter had driven her to on that day that now seemed like a lifetime ago, she looked at him in surprise. The Owner saw this and smiled.

In the elevator, the Owner turned the key that unlocked floor thirty. Shiny gold paneling covered the elevator's walls. It had been buffed to such a high sheen that it was almost a mirror. Cicely turned to see the reflection of her dress from a more provocative angle. She stuck out one leg, which revealed a knobby knee and an inch of thigh. The Owner was too busy fiddling with his cell phone to notice. He whispered to himself as he composed a text.

When the elevator groaned to a stop, the heavy doors slowly parted. Inch by inch, Cicely could see farther into the hushed and darkened golden space beyond. Soft carpet crawled away from the elevator and up to a small podium covered with thick fabric. Black drapes dangled along the walls, disappearing into a narrow corridor that angled back away behind the podium. Music and conversation filtered toward them from somewhere down that hall, but it was muffled. The drapes and carpet ate up every too-loud note and guffaw.

A fat man in a tuxedo stood at the podium, wearing an aggressive, fixed grin. He nodded when he saw the Owner: "Mr. Bangs, good evening." Cicely had never heard his real name before.

The Owner sent his text then looked up. "Booth please." While Cicely felt nervous in such gilded surroundings, the Owner acted dismissive and unimpressed.

The man in the tuxedo bowed and gestured toward the corridor. Cicely waited for the Owner to take a step, but he was waiting for her. After an awkward moment, she laughed and walked forward. Stepping into the hallway, the world hushed. All sound turned gauzy and unreal, and even her footsteps seemed too soft, as if she wasn't really walking. Traveling down the corridor felt like walking in a giant loop snaking upward. As she proceeded, the hallway grew darker and darker, till she could barely see the walls around her, but after a few more steps it began to lighten again and she eventually entered a small ballroom.

A massive glowing chandelier hung from the center of the ceiling, flanked by four smaller ones that burned in the corners of the room. The center of the space was sunk down and covered with round tables blanketed by white cloths. More heavy drapes lined the two sides of the room. Some of them hung open, revealing elevated booths. At the front of the room, on a small platform, a man in a tuxedo was whirling what looked like a giant spherical bird cage made out of gold. At the tables in the middle of the room, men in elegant suits and women in shiny gowns sat side by side, chatting and giggling or kissing and caressing each other. The tables themselves were cluttered with Champagne glasses, nibbled-at slices of chocolate cake, ivory cups filled with hot tea, and white cards on which sat gold tokens.

The host led Cicely and the Owner to one of the open booths on the left side of the room. As they walked, Cicely eyed the women at the tables below. As pretty as she felt, these women's propped-up cleavage, the slits in their skin-tight gowns, the spectacular three-dimensional gems they wore around their soft necks, all of it made her feel homely.

The man in the tuxedo onstage brought the twirling golden cage to a halt. As Cicely and the Owner stepped up into their booth, the man grasped a sphere that had bubbled to the top and held it aloft. "G forty-eight!" he cried. Many in the room groaned.

The table that separated Cicely and the Owner was narrow, crafted out of dark wood. On it lay two thick white cards, one for Cicely and one for the Owner, each bearing the letters B, I, N, G, and O across the top. Twenty-five hand-drawn squares filled the center of the cards, each containing one elegantly scripted numeral. To the side of each card lay a velvety pouch. Inside rested gold coins.

Cicely held her card up to the Owner. "Bingo?" She smirked. "What the fuck?"

The host was delivering glasses of Champagne. He frowned at Cicely's vulgarity.

"Have you played?" the Owner asked. "I thought you'd like it."

When the host was done serving the Champagne, he pulled the drapes closed, leaving behind a metal plate into which the night's menu had been etched. The Owner leaned over to the wall and turned a knob. Small speakers above transmitted the noise from the room and the stage into the dark interior of the booth. In the dim light, the Owner's tan face and neck looked maroon. The top two buttons of his shirt were undone, and Cicely could see a handful of small yellow hairs that grew in the exposed V. He leaned back and said nothing.

"N thirty-two!"

More groans.

Cicely wanted to wait for the Owner to speak first, but she couldn't stand the quiet between them. "I heard something about you," she blurted out.

It was like he didn't even hear her. "I like coming up here maybe once a month. Lots of those people out there are here every night. It can become an addiction." He fondled the heavy coins inside his velvet sack. "Too random for me. I only like playing games I can get better at." The bag thumped when he tossed it back on the table.

"Like golf?"

"God no." He snorted. "I said something I can get better at."

"When I was a kid, I loved soccer. Nothing organized—we couldn't afford that. I just played with kids in the neighborhood."

The Owner shook his head: "You don't see kids out playing anything anymore."

"Well, with the fish—"

"No, I mean even before that."

She hadn't thought about it before, and she'd never noticed it, the change had been so gradual, but yes the streets and fields had emptied years ago. "Don't go getting nostalgic on me," she said. "I get enough of that at work."

"The old-timers?"

"It's like they think they had nothing to do with anything. Like they weren't the ones in charge when everything went to shit."

"You think it's that bad, really?"

Was he blind? When he looked out the windows from the front seat of his car, or when he looked down from his office, or when he went boating, what did he see? Abandoned roads jagged with cracks, empty storefronts, lacerated shop windows, obscene graffiti, people sleeping on benches, crunched up into little balls because the benches had been designed to prevent people from sleeping on them, splattered armadillos around which crows clustered, rooftops that had been blown off, rooftops that had never been built, hunks of concrete that dropped from parking garages, fields once grass now just brown, invasive vines choking trees, downed power lines, dogs running loose nipping at people's heels, garbage cans blowing in the wind, scattered coffee grounds, banana peels, onion skins, Styrofoam, pizza boxes, gristle, fat, sinew, bone.

"I see your point," the Owner continued. "My dad is always complaining about kids having too much sex. Meanwhile he's on wife number three. And my half-brother was born when my dad was nineteen." His face clouded. "But somehow times were better back then. Right? More moral."

"My dad," Cicely said, "he's always saying, was always saying stuff like that. That when he was young, people acted right. People went to church, were nicer to one another. But did he ever go to church himself? Pffft. The only time we went to church was when St. Mark's handed out free food."

"Father Bill."

"Do you know him?"

The bubbles in the Owner's glass were evaporating. "He's active politically."

"So he's a real person. I never knew if he was from around here or if they piped in the video from somewhere else."

"O sixty-eight!"

A woman exclaimed wildly. "Bingo! Bingo!"

The Owner dumped the coins from his bag onto the table. "Finally. Now we can start a game."

"What do you win if you win?" Cicely asked. She too dumped out her tokens.

"Depends on the night. Could just be part of the pot of money or a new car or a title to something." He arranged his coins into a grid and brushed off the crisp Bingo card. "Feeling lucky tonight?"

"Never."

Through the speakers, Cicely could hear the man onstage once again begin turning the cage around and around. The golden balls rattled.

"You said you heard something about me." The Owner had turned up the light in the booth slightly so he could read the menu. He punched a button that summoned their server.

Cicely folded her hands and rested them in her lap. Her dress, already tight, suddenly felt constricting, as if she were being squeezed by a snake. The right shoulder strap cut into her skin. "I heard your golf course is to blame for all the dead fish." She still hadn't drunk any Champagne. She just rotated the slender glass with the tips of her fingers.

His lips met in an arrogant grimace.

Cicely cleared her throat: "I heard that runoff from there is what's killing the fish."

The Owner slammed a palm down on the table. "First that fucking lizard. They try to accuse us of that. Now the fish, too?"

Just as quickly as he exploded, he calmed. "I'm sorry. I'm not angry with you. I just…"

"I twenty-six!"

"It's just frustrating, that's all," the Owner said, looking at his card to see if he could place a coin. "We're just trying to fix up a golf course, that's all. But everybody wants to stick their noses in."

Cicely looked at her card. It didn't have a match. "Have you done any tests? You could prove them wrong."

He pushed his card away in disgust. "I'll never give them the satisfaction."

"Then how do you know that—"

"The last thing I wanted to do when I invited you out was to talk more about that golf course. After November, it won't be an issue."

"I'm sorry if I upset you." That was a lie—she felt gleeful. "I'm going to run to the restroom."

She swooped out of the booth. The man in the tuxedo had just pulled a new ball: "O seventy!" A few men and women pumped their fists.

There were no signs for the bathroom, but a server pointed Cicely in the right direction. She ducked behind a curtain and the door to the bathroom slid open.

Every tile in the restroom was red, every metal surface brushed nickel, and the doors to the toilets stretched all the way to the floor. Cicely heard a flush and a woman in an emerald gown emerged from one of the stalls. She brushed past Cicely without acknowledging her and set down her purse near the sinks.

When Cicely came out, the woman was gone, but she had left something behind: a folded rectangle of foil. Glancing around to make sure the bathroom was empty, Cicely crept up to the counter and delicately opened the silver pouch. Inside sat a small baggie loaded with round ivory pills—dozens of them. Cicely gasped and her heart began thumping. She had no idea what they were, but she could guess. She swiped as many as she thought she could take without the woman noticing, slipping the pills underneath the fabric around her breasts. She carefully closed the foil package so that it looked as if no one had touched it.

Neither Cicely nor the Owner won anything. When he dropped off Cicely after midnight, the Owner leaned over and kissed her on the cheek—nothing more—and said he'd like to do it again someday. "I'd like that," Cicely said, not meaning it, but not really lying either.

Zinnia was already in bed with her door closed, so Cicely stripped off the dress and laid it down next to her mattress, being careful to first remove the handful of pills. She placed them in the pages of *The Awakening* and put the book on the floor by her head. How much could she get for them? Was it worth trying to go to Dwayne with them? Or should she just eat them herself? She'd never tried drugs before. She never had enough money. She'd take food any day.

35.

She started riding the bus at random, waking and dressing for work early then meandering down to the nearest stop and hopping on whichever bus came first, not caring about the route, nor the destination. With her headphones on, she cut out the booming sound of the movies the drivers played and just sat staring out the window, resting sometimes on forearms crossed on the seat in front of her, leaning on her fist when she cocked her head toward the window.

The buses carried her deep into the eastern part of the county, well beyond the Interstate, past even the roomiest subdivisions and the largest mansions, where the neighborhoods—Savoy, Fox Acres Glen, Plantation Pines—faded out into actual pastureland, or what used to be pastureland, the grass here now mostly gray, the remaining cows bearing sharp rib lines on their sides. The bus line ended at a many-holed dirt parking lot next to a convenience store. You could either catch another line to continue on east, over to the other coast, or wait for one heading back to the city. Cicely would buy an ice cream sandwich from the store and walk in circles, listening to music and slurping at the treat. Occasionally a small jet would whine overhead, maybe an eighteen-wheeler would barrel by. But other than that, it was quiet.

On its way back into town, the bus passed the golf course. She recognized the name—Wolf Glen—from chatter at work. In truth, it barely looked like a course. Its driveway lay hidden beneath powerful vines and yawning sand cavities had opened up in the green floor of the one tee box she could see from the road. Yard-thick roots clamped down on whatever vegetation remained and a water hazard near the road bubbled over with filthy orange ooze. On the bank lay an alligator, long dead, with a gash running up its stomach and its guts hanging out. Dead birds lay in a circle around the body. This was where her father had ended up.

Cicely rode south, too, down where there were no buildings taller than three stories, where the neighborhoods flattened out and the streets circled around in strange curlicues that led nowhere. One of the bus lines stopped at a jetty on which men wearing surgical masks sat with lines in the water. Clumps of dead fish had washed up in the corner where the jetty met the beach; a brown foam surged out from the corpses.

Another southern bus line dropped her outside a mall, abandoned except for a Radio Shack, its shelves nearly empty. She walked the empty food court, ran her hand along the metal shutters that hid the old shops, climbed onto one of the plastic horses on the now-still carousel. Some kids must have started a bonfire inside—a pile of charred furniture and half-melted mannequins lay in one corner, surrounded by smashed bottles and stamped-out cigarette butts.

Cicely didn't care where she was, didn't care what she was looking at. She just rode and walked. Something inside her had broken apart.

She kept the bus schedule in her back pocket, always aware that she needed to end up near the dance hall in time for her shift. When Zinnia asked where she was going, or where she had gone, or why she was so unhappy, Cicely couldn't formulate a real answer, just mumbled something about the sky out east or the pleasure of the headphones or the rumble of the bus.

Up north, the bus left her at a rec center in the middle of five trailer parks. It was a Saturday, school was out, and boys huddled around a big TV, taking turns with the two controllers connected to the rec center's old video game console. The game was out-of-date—a football simulation with teams that no longer played in the same cities as when the game had been designed. Cicely sat in the back, her music paused, listening to the click-click-tap-tap-click of teenaged boys' fingers on buttons and the hisses from the kids watching when someone made a big play.

The girls sat in a circle away from the TV, turning their heads whenever one of the boys screamed or cursed, but otherwise paying them no mind. They combed one another's hair, they leaned their heads on shoulders, they took turns telling stories and giggling. None of them gave Cicely a second look, none of them thought it odd that here was a grown-up adult sitting there watching them.

She left the rec center and walked the narrow lanes of the surrounding trailer parks. Laundry was strung up along lines that stretched from unit to unit, and wall air-conditioners buzzed in the corridors where windows faced windows, with curtains made from old T-shirts that offered the barest hint of privacy.

Blinding white shells lined the pathways that rounded in and out of the dense network of mobile homes. The wind kicked up chalky white dust that coated Cicely's feet. At home, after her shift, late at night, she soaked them in the tub. The warm water grew rich and milky.

36.

Her mother finally wrote back.

> *C.,*
> *I'm here.*
> *M.*

But now, with no pickups to make and work slow as shit, Cicely couldn't afford to take time off. One night, the hall hosted a modern dance performance, just a man in gray shorts and a woman in a gray smock, their muscles bulging so much that the man and woman were difficult to tell apart, the woman with what looked like muscles on her shoulder blades, muscles Cicely didn't even know existed, and the man with carved shoulders and arms. They danced on an empty stage, all black except for a box of light that seemed to contain them. The music droned. It sounded to Cicely like someone just scraping guitar strings for minutes on end, but it entranced Zinnia, who watched the whole show from a table in the back. The music, so atonal, felt so different from Zinnia's warm chords. Cicely wondered what she heard in it.

"It's not trying to please," Zinnia said. "It's telling people to sit here. Endure this."

The dancers moved in such a way that Cicely couldn't tell if their actions were spontaneous or choreographed. First the woman fell then was caught then rose again then fell again then leapt then twisted on the floor. During the second act, the music was accompanied by a vocal snippet. The words came from a flight attendant; she was telling you how to buckle your seat belt. But the audio was slowed way, way down and played over and over again, then phased in and out till it was really two voices that slowly separated then slowly came back together till they were both in sync for one final phrase. The dance ceased.

Most of the room applauded gently. Zinnia clapped furiously then left without saying goodbye to Cicely, who was stuck pouring Mai Tais for another couple hours. The clientele for the dance performance was less boisterous than the regulars, their conversations conducted at low volume. Cicely had to lean low while pouring to eavesdrop.

When Cicely saw Dwayne step outside to smoke, she followed him. He paced in circles around the parking lot while he tapped his pack of cigarettes. Cicely never knew why smokers did that.

She called out to him. He paused, licking his lips and spinning a cigarette between his fingers. "Looking for something?" he asked.

He thought she was just another buyer; this annoyed her. "Probably not what you think," she said. She stepped down into the parking lot and sauntered over to him. The breeze felt cool along the outside of her breasts. She hooked her thumbs into the waistband of her tights, fingered the plastic bag with the pills inside. She had taken to carrying them wherever she went so Zinnia wouldn't find them at home. "I'm looking for capital," she said.

His brow wrinkled. "Like a loan? Get the fuck out." He still hadn't lit his cigarette, just kept twisting it in his hand.

Cicely felt the urge to spit a thick wad on the ground, but refrained. "Like a sale."

Dwayne looked over his shoulders. The lot was empty. The surface of the retention pond rippled in the wind. "How much you got?"

"Not much." She thought she was playing it cool, but was she? "Twelve pills or so."

"Not much, you're right."

Why not lie? "There will be more to come."

"I'd be suspicious, but it's pretty easy to tell you're not wearing a wire." He pointed at her bare chest.

"There's no incentive for either of us to say anything."

"You've got a point." He looked at his hands and made some calculations on his fingers. "Five hundred." When she looked at him skeptically he raised a hand in defense. "That's a friend price."

"So we're friends now?"

"Give me a couple days."

As Cicely walked back inside, she heard the click of his lighter behind her.

Delanna was pissed off when Cicely walked back on the floor: "Where have you been?" She was sloppily pouring Mai Tais, with half the room calling for more. Cicely glared at her, grabbed a pitcher, and went back to work.

37.

Good news: Anna established a new connection, to the north, and no one would have to go to any actual hospital anymore. But the drive took longer, up a weed-cluttered road that tracked along the bigger bay to the north, and the new nurse wanted to meet twice a week. "It's perfect for you two, perfect for you two," Anna told Cicely and Zinnia, laughing in that choking, high-pitched way of hers.

Neither Cicely nor Zinnia wanted to go alone the first time, so they piled into the van and made the trip together. Zinnia volunteered to drive the first leg. The road bumped and humped, jostling the two of them and rattling the van. Cicely had hooked her CD player up to the stereo, but the constant jerks up and down kept making the CDs skip.

The promise of good money lifted Zinnia's mood; she sang along to the music when she knew the lyrics and told stories about the one time she went out on tour with a band she had formed with kids from music school. Cicely mumbled replies. She too was happy about the prospect of fresh cash, but something about Anna's laugh unsettled her. Did anything ever happen to Lisa, the pink-haired nurse? Had the hospital really just cut the cord with her? Left it at that?

After the crash, the government shut off most of the streetlights outside the cities. One advantage was that you could see more stars than ever before, particularly out in the middle of nowhere. Even with the headlights shining on the road in front of them, Cicely could see a whole blanket of twinkling lights above the tree line, shining from points so far away it made Cicely's stomach twist just thinking about it, that old question—why anything?—skipping to the realization that without anything, we wouldn't be here wondering, an answer in no way satisfying, even more nauseating in a way, the marginal blip of life somehow an excuse for all this around her. After the streetlights went dark, it was common to hear people chattering about how beautiful the stars were, but to Cicely they weren't beautiful. They were reminders of the insignificance of her life, carrying inside them the affirmation that one day her life would end and it would not make the slightest difference.

Zinnia's old band was a furious all-female punk quartet, their singer notorious for leaping into the crowd, licking audience members' faces, and screaming into their ears. The problem: they had three fans, max, which took away from the impact of her launching herself from the stage. Zinnia didn't sing, just played bass and bored through the audience with an indifferent gaze. She was telling Cicely a story about one time when a guy in a cowboy hat punched the singer in the face and the singer had to go to the hospital because she was bleeding so badly but then they refused to treat her because it was obvious she was broke. The story sounded horrible to Cicely, but Zinnia told it like a joke.

The road narrowed, as if the trees were closing in on them. In the dark, the vegetation looked blue.

"It's hard to picture you in a punk band," Cicely said. "You don't seem angry."

Zinnia looked in the rearview mirror. "Always." When the van bumped, so did her crimped hair. "I just hide it well."

Cicely wanted to tell her, "Not really," that it was pretty easy to see that Zinnia had been pissed at her ever since her date with the Owner, but she didn't want to spoil Zinnia's good mood.

The headlights drifted over yellow line, yellow line, yellow line, the ditches on either side of the road just long strips of inky shadows. About an hour after they set out, they arrived at the meeting spot: a long-ago-shuttered Arby's, its tall hat-shaped sign still intact but dark. Zinnia pulled the van around behind the restaurant. The box into which customers once shouted their orders hung limply to the side. A giant green dumpster sat on the concrete out back. A sticky brown sludge pooled underneath it. It was a strange place to meet, but it was also the only thing close to a landmark Cicely and Zinnia had passed in at least twenty miles. Zinnia switched off the engine; she and Cicely both rolled down their windows. The live oaks that surrounded the parking lot waved gently. A possum, gone haywire, spun in circles in the middle of the concrete.

In a few moments, they heard the tender crunch of wheels on pavement. An old maroon sedan, one headlight busted, emerged from around the opposite side of the building and slowly wheeled over to them. A dude in blue nursing scrubs hopped out, rubbing the stubble on his shaved head. He raised a hand.

Cicely stepped out and waved back. She felt intensely aware of her surroundings. The metal frame of the van door was so cold, the concrete beneath her feet pebbled and raw. The stars hummed. Zinnia left the van, too. Cicely felt her at her side.

The nurse opened the trunk of the red car and came up with a bag just like the ones Cicely used to catch at the hospital. Something didn't feel right. Would the bag really be exactly the same? The nurse, too—this man did not look like someone who worked in the mother-baby unit. He walked over and held out the bag. Zinnia took it. As Zinnia walked to the back of the van, Cicely and the nurse just stared at each other. The stubble wasn't confined to his head. It crawled down past his ears and to his chin, coating his fat neck. The bottom of his shirt didn't quite cover his belly, and his pants sagged so much Cicely could see where the giant roll of his stomach attached to his waist. Even his ears were ugly, just lumps of gristle stuck to his potato-shaped skull.

The rear doors of the van slammed shut. Cicely didn't want to turn her back on this guy, who just kept standing there, watching her and rubbing his stomach, but it was time to go. She gingerly stepped backward and up into the driver's seat, keeping her eyes fixed on the nurse. Even when she fired up the van and flicked on the lights the guy didn't flinch. As she pulled out of the parking lot and back onto the main road, she looked back. The nurse had turned his head and was watching them leave. His glare left her frosty. She wanted to tell Zinnia she was worried, but she was afraid to. Zinnia would say she was acting childish.

Back on the road, wheels spinning, Cicely started to forget the nurse. She settled her gaze on the faded yellow strips lit up by the headlights and watched out for potholes. She put on some Joni and didn't even mind that the bumps kept interrupting the songs. Zinnia slipped off her sandals and laid her legs up on the dash. She kept rubbing her left ankle with her right foot, absently humming along to the music. She unbuttoned her shirt down to her belly button to fight the heat.

Headlights. In the rearview mirror, Cicely saw headlights. Just two distant white points, but growing larger. Her chest clutched her heart. Who would be out at this hour? On this road? Police? She checked the speedometer. Was she speeding? No. Before each run, Cicely always checked her taillights, even checked the lights that illuminated the license plate—she knew they were all working. If it was cops, they had no reason to pull them over. But did that matter? Cicely knew the police could do whatever they wanted.

Zinnia had seen the lights, too, and watched them in her side mirror. She and Cicely looked each other in the eyes, both their faces flushed with panic and lit up with sharp white light. And then, from behind, came the spinning red. Cicely gasped. Without thinking, she slowed the van.

"No no no," Zinnia said, grabbing Cicely's arm. "Speed up."

"We can't outrun him."

"Go go go." Zinnia reached a foot over as if she would stomp on the gas if Cicely didn't. "We can't get caught."

Cicely pushed the speed over the limit. The headlights raced right behind them.

Cicely: "Oh fuck…" Oh no, oh no. Where did they go? She began digging in her pants.

"What?" Zinnia's voice, normally so low, had turned sharp. "What?"

There. Cicely felt the lip of the bag with the pills. It had slipped from the front of her waistband around to the side. She yanked it from her pants and held it in her right palm, low, below the headlights, so Zinnia could see. Cicely's face grew wet with tears.

"Are you fucking kidding me with that?" Zinnia's voice turned vengeful. "Are you serious? What the fuck are you doing with those? Oh my fucking Lord." She put her fingers to her forehead.

"At the Bingo hall—"

"I don't want to hear it. I do not want to hear it." Zinnia's feet were on the floor of the van now, twitching up and down. "It doesn't matter now." She chewed on a knuckle. "Think. Think."

The cop's siren blared.

"Get the placentas," Cicely said. "We'll have to run."

Zinnia unclicked her seatbelt and climbed into the rear of the van. They hit a pothole and jerked to the right. Zinnia slipped. Her head banged against the side of the vehicle. Woozed, she got back to her knees and crawled over to the cooler. The cop's headlights swerved back and forth, the creamy beams twisting strange shadows up and down the van's walls. Cicely heard the cooler open and close, and there was Zinnia, crawling back to her seat, clutching the green bag.

The vegetation on the side of the road thinned out in this stretch, the dense moss-clad oaks giving way to open scrub land, wide prairies carpeted with stubby saw palms and intersected with mammoth roots and dotted with Florida rosemary, with skinny pine trees stretching up toward the stars. A tiny scrape of moon hung near the horizon. Darkness rested over everything.

Cicely eased up on the gas, the van slowing to thirty. "Get ready to run," she said, undoing her seatbelt. "Get as far out as you can then get down and stay down." She slowed the van even more and watched the rearview mirror.

The headlights behind them swung left and right, the cop annoyed. After a few moments, finally, the car cut into the left lane and accelerated. The cop was trying to draw even. At just that moment, Cicely slammed on the brakes. As the van screeched to a halt she and Zinnia threw open their doors and bolted out into the prairie.

Roots battered ankles. Palm fronds tore shins. Branches ripped forearms. Cicely panted. Zinnia moaned. Cicely heard the cop's brakes squeal. "Down!" Zinnia shouted. They both leapt into the underbrush. Cicely's stomach crashed into an arm-thick root. She gasped. Zinnia's hand clamped down over her mouth.

Everything quiet now. Cicely could hear the clop-clop of the cop's boots. They sounded so near. Cicely and Zinnia had barely made it out into the prairie, but the low growth was so thick there was no way the cop could see them. Cicely tried to look through palms back to the road, to see where the cop was, but the plants grew so dense she couldn't see more than a few feet. She looked up instead. The sky was pocked with stars.

Cicely could feel Zinnia's heart racing in the fingers that closed across her face. She gently pushed Zinnia's hand away. The cop's boots scuffed along the road, to the left, to the right. The beam of a flashlight crawled across the prairie, its milky glow edging closer to where Cicely and Zinnia lay. The light fingered the palms above them, flaring their deep green fronds, turning them almost translucent, bright and silvery, making Cicely think the light could burn through everything around her, could turn it all to ash, then settle on her, the circle of light growing hot, hotter, till her skin would turn purple and red and flake away. But the circle of light passed over them and drifted away to the south. Cicely heard the cop rumbling in the van, heard the cooler lid snap open then shut. Warm dirt crept into the waist of Cicely's jeans; a rock cut into her exposed lower back. Her hand found Zinnia's; their fingers folded together.

How lazy was this cop? This was the most pressing question. Was it really worth his time to wade out into the prairie—

risking twisted ankle, lost cell phone, snakebite—to come after them? Would the cop stay in his car all night, waiting for them to come out, make some kind of noise? Since the crash, every cop Cicely came across had struck her as indifferent, their one job to make sure people didn't panhandle, didn't congregate, didn't sleep in the parks the city didn't want them to sleep in. Aside from that, you could pretty much do what you wanted.

But hardasses remained, she was sure. A year ago, Delanna told her a story about a cop who caught her boyfriend urinating on the beach and beat him senseless, and Hilda had once been arrested and slapped after she stole packets of soy sauce from the grocery store. But this cop didn't just randomly happen upon them. Someone had set them up. That was obvious. Had the pink-haired nurse squealed? Had the hospital decided to inform the police? Anna? The suspicion hit Cicely with a thud, but it didn't make much sense. What did Anna have to gain? Wasn't she losing out, too, if Cicely and Zinnia were locked up? Less money for all of them. Maybe she was cutting her losses, sacrificing them. The photo of the woman with the punctured face flashed in front of Cicely's eyes.

She was so wrapped up in her thoughts that Zinnia had to nudge her to make her hear the cop's car start up and then putter away. Cicely raised her head just over the lip of palms. The car drifted slowly back in the direction they had come from, the flashlight beam shining from the driver's side window and creeping over the landscape. It swung toward her. She ducked. Brakes squeaked. No. No. No. Zinnia squeezed Cicely's hand so tightly pain cascaded up her arm. Again, they held their breath. The flashlight illuminated the palms above them and rested there, blotting out the sky. Cicely tried to freeze every cell in her body.

After a few moments, the flashlight drifted away and the sound of the car's engine once again receded. Being careful not to rise above the level of vegetation, Cicely rolled onto her side, trying to find a soft spot in which to lie. Her gut felt bruised. Lying on her side, she could see Zinnia, who was also wiggling, trying to locate a comfortable spot. A car engine zoomed down the road, going in the direction in which Cicely and Zinnia had originally been headed. After a moment, silence again descended. The two walked out deeper into the woods and lay down in a hollow amid the palms.

Cicely whispered: "Should we wait here?"

Zinnia nodded. One of her hands still clutched Cicely's; the other was wrapped around the bag of placentas. Indicating the bag, she whispered back: "At least we won't go hungry."

Cicely laughed. She shook her head in wonder. How the hell did I get here? Her eyes met Zinnia's. Zinnia's hair was a wild tangle, her face streaked with soil.

38.

A rustle in the palms woke her. Without thinking, she jerked upright. Morning had come in the form of a fuzzy gray fog. She looked around. The van still sat on the road, both doors yawning. No one in sight.

Whatever had woken her up just kept moving, crashing through branches and leaves, till it was right next to her. She parted two palms to look. The armadillo didn't even notice her, just kept barreling through the field, its striped hide bending back branches. Cicely gripped her forehead with both hands. Her brain ached. As if her worst hangover had been multiplied by ten.

High above, four turkey vultures circled. Cicely sniffed something terrible, something like rotting flesh. Oh God, the placentas. The stink must have attracted the birds. The bag had slipped from Zinnia's hands and lay in the dirt. Maggots and flies squirmed all over it. When Cicely picked it up, she was so disgusted she almost vomited. A cockroach climbed up her wrist. She flinched and chucked the bag as far as she could. She brushed the bug off her and shivered.

Zinnia had somehow slept through all this, so Cicely just sat back down and waited for her to wake up. As the morning light intensified, Zinnia's face scrunched up, lines creasing around her eyes, like her mind was trying to squeeze something out, then her eyelids parted and she rubbed the drool from her mouth and she was awake.

"God, my head." She massaged her temples as she high-stepped away a few feet. She pulled down her pants, squatted, and pissed. "Where'd the bag go?"

Cicely pointed in the direction in which she'd thrown it. "It had defrosted."

Pulling up her jeans: "Lunch for somebody, I guess."

Cicely nodded toward the van. "Think it's safe to drive?"

Zinnia shook her head.

They walked, following the road back to town and crouching down in the bushes whenever they heard a car. After an hour they found a convenience store and bought water and chips. After another hour they saw the outskirts of the city, the first neatly clipped lawns and guard gates, the scripted subdivision signs. Afraid of going home, they caught a bus to the dance hall, where they showered and changed and ate and waited for Dwayne. He showed up at four and paid Cicely five hundred for the pills. With a hundred, they bought two roundtrip bus tickets.

39.

Orlando.

As the bus pulled into the station, it occurred to Cicely she had been here before. Her parents couldn't afford tickets to the big theme parks, but they had once come to an old water park here. She had been maybe eight or nine. Her father hadn't come to the park with them—he had won a ticket to a football game. Yes, that's why they had gone to Orlando. Her father had won a ticket for some bowl game and they had all taken the bus up for a weekend, she and her mother heading to the water park while her father attended the game.

How had she forgotten that? She loved it. Her mother was content to sit quietly in an inner tube and float on the lazy river that cut through the park, while Cicely climbed the huge towers that took her to the tops of the daunting slides. Everything smelled like chlorine, even the food, and she remembered how her bathing suit would grow cold and cling to her stomach while she waited in line, the chill strange on such a hot day, and how it felt so good at the end of the day to wrap herself in one of the park's oversized towels and sit quietly next to her mother drinking a Coke that tasted more sugary than any Coke she had ever tasted before.

The bus station, with its long bays and glass-enclosed ticket counter, brought this all back to Cicely in an instant, the sensation so strong it felt like rubbing the warm terrycloth along her shivering arms all over again. The station at night was still, the quiet punctuated by an occasional squirt of air from an idling bus. Cicely and Zinnia walked out to the street, where men held up pictures of cheap motels and shouted prices and amenities at them. They picked the cheapest spot and piled into a white minivan that took them to the motel, where they checked in and immediately collapsed.

The next day they ate soggy bacon and fake eggs in the motel breakfast nook, gulping down acidic coffee and pulp-less orange juice. Only when they got up to leave did they realize they had no plan. They collected brochures from the fake wood rack by the check-in counter and strolled back to their room. Cicely's head still ached from sleeping out in the field; the bright sunshine made everything worse, filling her face with pain.

In the room, she and Zinnia pulled the curtains shut and climbed back into bed and flicked on the TV using the remote chained to the nightstand. Cicely had gotten used to living without a television, but when one was around she couldn't resist turning it on, and once it was on, she couldn't resist staring at it, even if she was ignoring someone right in front of her. The morning news team was discussing a new sex tape involving the governor. Would it hurt him politically, with the election right around the corner?

It was delicious to have nowhere to be, no responsibilities. At some point, Cicely fell back into a deep sleep then woke again then fell asleep once more. Zinnia too drifted in and out of wakefulness. When Cicely finally felt fully conscious, it was already early afternoon, and the TV was still on. The commentators were discussing the governor's tape, analyzing his performance.

After Cicely took a shower, she wrapped her hair in a beige towel and waited for Zinnia to come to. She had no desire to hunt for her mother just yet. That needed a fresh day, a day when she felt whole and ready rather than sore and shattered. She stared at the pixels of the television, but she wasn't paying attention to the news, was instead wondering if she had thrown everything away. Could she and Zinnia go home? Would Anna be looking for them? Or the cops? Could she keep her job at the dance hall? The manager had seemed cool with them taking off for a few days, but they couldn't push their luck. Surely some young woman was applying for her job right now, some woman who was friendlier, less jaded. There were millions of Cicelys out there; nothing made her special. Zinnia was special—you couldn't count on someone else having her talent. But even her: would she have anything to go back to? Would her fans abandon her? Just take up some other singer, someone who sang hits from the movies? Had they lost everything? But what did that even mean—what was it worth, after all? They had survived, that was it, that was all their previous life had offered them. But then there were those moments, late at night, when she and Zinnia would be sitting around the house, drinking, talking, singing dumb songs. The dance hall, the placentas, they had given her that, she supposed, they had allowed her that. She knew she should be more grateful; people had been telling her that since she was a girl. Be grateful. Be grateful. You're lucky. To have a job, to have a family, to not be dead. Zinnia erupted in fury whenever someone suggested she be grateful, but as horrible as Cicely's days generally were, she did at times feel lucky. Here she was, sitting on a bed with a friend sleeping next to her, her hair clean and drying in the towel twisted upon her head, her toes wiggling down there at the end of her feet, almost four hundred bucks still tucked into the pocket of her jeans, thrown over the back of the chair over there by the front window. Her thoughts drifted away. As she watched TV, her hand slipped beneath her towel and her fingers twisted her pubic hair.

The realization she might see her mother any day now hit her. She tried to picture what her mother might look like, what her expression might be when she recognized Cicely, but she couldn't. That photo of her mother in the tire swing was all Cicely could see: those sun-touched cheeks dotted with light brown freckles, the piles of buoyant curls that jiggled above her head, those slightly chubby legs in those fraying denim cutoffs. What year was that photo from? Cicely had probably been eight or nine, meaning her mother was sixteen, seventeen years older than that now. Had she aged well? What kind of work did she do? Had it left a mark on her? Slipping back into sleep, Cicely pictured the moment she would meet her. She looked beautiful, even more radiant than in the photo, dressed in a soft flower-print dress that fell to her knees, strands of pearls dangling around her neck, her brown shoulders still big, bare, her teeth white, her face untroubled by lines or rings or splotches, her embrace so warm, her hug so firm, the two squeezed together into one whole. Then the invitation, the request. "Please come stay with me," her mother said dreamily. "Please come to my home." The sound of those words made Cicely tingle. Out of nowhere came this desire to be scooped up, to be carried with one strong arm behind her head and one beneath her knees. She looked up into her mother's face. She became a child, a baby.

Evening came. Hunger forced Cicely and Zinnia to move, pushing them out the door and into the tangle of streets around them. Downtown itself was empty, its dark thoroughfares just hollow swelling canyons. An enormous broadcasting tower, once fixed to the roof of a nearby TV station, had collapsed, blocking one street entirely. Cracks had popped open in the pavement; grass and wildflowers sprang up.

Finally they saw signs of life: young kids running in wild circles around an overgrown park that sat in the middle of a cluster of banks. Parents sat on benches that ringed the park, eating gyros from foil packages. A food cart sat in the far corner of the park; its flattop sizzled with meat and spilled a salty, greasy mist into the air. When Cicely and Zinnia placed their order, the red-haired guy running the cart shaved off long strips of meat from a spit and then heated them up on the stove top. Cicely and Zinnia found spots on one of the red benches and settled in to eat. The parents near them gave them a strange look. Somehow, they could tell Cicely and Zinnia were outsiders, as if it were written on their forehead: stranger.

The playground equipment inside the park was rusting away and had even broken apart at points, but that didn't faze the kids. They clambered up and over half-destroyed monkey bars and zoomed down plastic slides with jagged edges. As Cicely watched, one little girl in overalls climbed over the railing of a bridge that spanned from one section of the playground to another. Her face radiated fear, nothing in front of her but space and the ground. But she jumped, screaming, her hands flailing, and she landed on her feet and then tumbled forward onto her knees. When she looked up, her huge smile seemed directed right at Cicely, who was mashing dough and meat and onion in her mouth.

"Would you ever want a kid?" she asked Zinnia.

Zinnia sucked cold tea through a straw. "Why do it to them? Make them go through this?"

Cicely felt the same, but Zinnia sounded more confident, more final. Cicely jabbed her in the upper arm with her finger. "Oh come on. It's not so bad." She laughed.

"Not right now, no," Zinnia said. She wiped yogurt from her lips with a finger and sucked till it was clean. "If nothing else, we've had a hell of an adventure."

"Yeah, fucking Orlando, right?"

The old woman on the bench next to Cicely turned her head at the obscenity. "Sorry," Cicely whispered, putting her head down. But she turned a hidden smile to Zinnia, who laughed quietly.

"Fucking Orlando!" Zinnia shouted, loud enough that even some of the kids on the playground turned their heads.

"We're going to get kicked out," Cicely said. She finished her gyro and balled up the foil. She stretched her legs out on the ground in front of her, feeling her muscles and tendons pull.

Still chewing, Zinnia smushed her foil into a ball, too, and pointed to a trashcan that stood twenty feet away. She raised the foil in her right hand and shot it toward the can like a basketball. It hit the rim of the can, bounced once, then skipped over the hole and down onto the ground. "Your turn," she said.

Cicely gauged the distance, moving her arm up and down, practicing her form.

Zinnia rolled her eyes. "Oh, just shoot—"

Cicely chucked the foil ball. It didn't land anywhere close to the trashcan. She must have overshot it by ten feet. "You distracted me," she said.

They left the park without bothering to pick up their garbage. Nighttime had fallen and the city had grown dark. "You know what I like about Orlando?" Zinnia asked, her head little more than an outline in the blue-green shadows. "No dead fish."

40.

It was easier than Cicely would have liked to get a lead on her mother. Using the motel phone book, she called a random post office and asked which location would have the PO number her mother used, and incredibly enough, they helped her and gave her the address with no hassle. Part of her hoped it would be a challenge, maybe even impossible, something she could attempt to do but fail at but still feel good about trying to do. But no— basically all she had to do now was sit at the post office all day and wait for her mother to show up. She ruled out doing it right away, because the post office had already been open for half an hour and by the time she got over there it would be even later and what if her mother was the type of early riser who got to her PO box first thing in the morning and Cicely missed her. So yes, safer to wait till tomorrow, catch a bus and get to the post office right when it opened.

With the stakeout delayed, Cicely and Zinnia lay in bed like slugs for a second day, this time talking back to the television. The breaking news was that it was the governor's own wife who shot the sex tape. Cicely hit mute and she and Zinnia offered their commentary. Around midday, Zinnia slipped out and down the street to the liquor store. She came back with a dusty bottle of Pernod the clerk had sold to her for a buck. "He said this exact bottle has been sitting on the same shelf since he started working there," Zinnia said, "twenty years ago." Cicely got ice from the hallway and they spent the afternoon mixing the booze with water, sipping it clear and sipping it milky.

At night they found a putt-putt course and played several rounds. The course was pirate-themed and the holes wound around several waterfalls and a pond in the front where a dozen or so baby alligators lived. You could pay a buck for a handful of food pellets to throw to them. The scene was way sad. The gators looked gaunt and agitated; the water they swam in had been polluted with so much dye that it resembled Gatorade. Cicely had never played putt-putt before and was surprised to discover a knack for the game, reading uneven greens and knocking her ball around blind curves with grace. Zinnia got grumpy after losing three games. She refused to believe Cicely had never played. After Cicely won a fourth round, Zinnia took both their clubs and launched them over the fence that ringed the course. When the teenaged kid who rented them the equipment came out to yell, they ran, splashing through the turquoise-colored creeks and pools and back to the road.

41.

Cicely didn't want Zinnia around when she first saw her mother. She caught the bus the next morning alone.

The post office sat just west of downtown, in an immense concrete lot protected by concertina wire. Right at eight in the morning, the fence rolled open and stubby trucks began pulling out. Cicely walked inside. The main building was constructed out of white-painted bricks; the linoleum inside was scabby and curling. Cicely walked down a long bank of mailboxes. Her fingertips trailed along the boxes' blocky metal, the small locks beat up and scratched from years of use. Cicely knew it was ridiculous, but the space felt holy in some way, all by her lonesome, just her and these boxes that carried bills, gifts, garbage, and love letters—and one of these boxes belonged to her mother, whom she hadn't seen in a decade. She hopped up onto a desk that held envelopes and boxes and a scale to weigh your packages. She hopped up and waited.

And waited. She didn't anticipate the boredom of sitting in a room waiting for someone to maybe walk in. No one came in to check any of the boxes in the first hour. After another thirty minutes, Cicely paced. A half-hour after that she skipped from floor tile to floor tile, trying to see how many she could jump at once. And then it was still just ten o'clock. The post office stayed open till six.

The first person she saw actually open a PO box was a guy so thin it looked like he might snap in two. The second person was a surfer-looking dude with a backward baseball cap and high tops. The third person was an old lady, way too old to be her mother, bent over and shuffling. She needed help just twisting the key in the lock. Nobody seemed happy with anything they received—mostly junk mail and bills, Cicely guessed, based on their disappointed faces. Were they expecting birthday cards? Letters from family oversees? Whatever it was they sought, they went away sad, each and every one.

At lunchtime, Cicely went across the street and ate a hot dog from a cart, keeping her eyes on the door to the post office. Most people entered with packages or envelopes and left empty-handed—none of them seemed the right age. She kept a closer eye on the ones who exited the building with fresh mail.

Which. There was a woman. Maybe fifty. But that couldn't be her. She walked outside, wrapped in a billowing muumuu with drawings of ice cream cones on it. Her ankles settled into jelly sandals below the hem of her dress. Her hair was curly, as Cicely's mother's had been, but it had grayed. Cicely narrowed her eyes. Could it be. The woman sorted through a small stack of papers, her face as crushed as everyone else's. She didn't get what she wanted.

Cicely skipped across the street. Her heart thudded. She steadied herself by grabbing onto the fence that surrounded the parking lot and watched the woman. Her mother, she was sure. At this moment, she was sure. She watched the woman walk toward the bus stop on the other side of the lot. Her back faced Cicely. Cicely pranced to catch up to her. She felt like a little girl. For a few moments, maybe ten, fifteen seconds, she walked behind her, watching her dress shake in the wind. The sun stood almost directly overhead; it burned through Cicely's hair, into her skull.

Should she tap her shoulder? Yell at her? Still strolling behind the woman, she leaned in and sniffed. Could she smell her mother? Could she tell it was her body? She had come from this body, after all. She had once been cells inside this body, then had grown hands, feet, a head, had been squeezed out of this body. This body had suffered to make her. But Cicely could detect no trace of that scent. The sweet smell of the woman's fabric softener was too strong.

"Why are you following me?" The woman's head swiveled around.

Her sharp tone startled Cicely. She jumped back a few inches. She paused. Her eyes widened. That face. It was her mother. Her cheeks had fattened, the creases branching out from her eyes had become more defined, her hair had passed from blond to gray-brown, but this was her mother's face. Yesterday's idle fantasy of being scooped up, of being carried around like a baby, looking up into this face, nuzzling in the crook of this neck, flashed through Cicely's mind. Her flesh tingled.

"Cicely."

It was a matter-of-fact statement—no warmth, no joy. Perhaps she had been burned before, had thought she had seen Cicely at the post office only to be disappointed.

Cicely nodded and threw her arms out, stepping forward and wrapping them around her mother. To feel her so close, to be touching her skin—the intensity of the moment was almost too much. Cicely shook. In return, her mother lightly patted Cicely on the shoulders. Cicely pulled back for a second and looked again at her mother's face: no tears, no smile, just a there-there kind of sympathy.

Gripping her tightly again, Cicely buried her face in her mother's shoulder, her tears wetting the blue fabric of the ice cream muumuu. But as happy as she felt, even in this moment, which she had dreamed of ever since the morning she found her father alone and had realized her mother had gone, as good as it felt to hold this woman close to her, something still wasn't right, in the way no moment ever felt like she wanted it to, the way loss and loneliness tinged everything. Like seeing a mouth-watering steak on a plate then taking a bite and realizing, Oh it's food, just food. For ten years Cicely dreamed of this hug, and now here she stood, squeezing a middle-aged woman who barely squeezed her back. Did she sob because she was meeting her mother again, or because even this experience, like every other one in her life, was letting her down? She released her mother and covered her face with her hands. Wherever she went, disappointment lurked.

Her mother seemed unsure what to do. She passed the small bundle of envelopes she had retrieved from her mailbox from her left hand to her right and back again. She scratched her left calf with the toes of her right foot. Cicely wanted to scream. Say something. Invite me somewhere. Take me away.

Cicely felt her mother's fleshy hand on her arm. "Cicely," she whispered. "We're going to miss the bus." She prodded Cicely over toward the curb and down the street to where a metal pole marked the bus stop. Old men used brown packages as seats. Teenagers stared angrily at everything, the heavy metal in their headphones turned up so loud everyone else could hear. Men in coveralls kept anxiously eying the clock that hung on the outside of the post office. No one gave Cicely's still-soaked face and red eyes and heaving chest a second glance. Most days, somebody did some crying here.

The bus didn't have AC. It was in fact an old repurposed school bus, painted white instead of yellow. The dark green vinyl that covered the long bench seats became blistering hot in the sun, burning Cicely's legs and drawing out sweat from her thighs. Between her now-sticky jeans, the ripe flavor emanating from her underarms, the acidic residue in her mouth from too much coffee, Cicely knew she stunk, was almost ashamed that this was how she smelled this morning of all mornings. Her mother grew sweaty, too, and kept fanning her neck and the open flesh around her collarbone with her stack of mail. All the windows on the bus were down; at the very least the hot breeze from the road kept Cicely's forehead dry.

Cicely's mother lived in a tall, boxy building set among five others in a giant sandy lot not too far from the post office. As they trudged across the burning sand, her mother told her the story of the neighborhood's construction, although Cicely could have probably guessed how these concrete monsters came to be. Before the crash, the city had voted to evict the tenants of a downtown building, calling the property a prime location for redevelopment. But the city promised to relocate all those affected, which of course meant building these tenements—that's what they were, really—way far away from everyone decent. The crash ruined everything. Only four out of six planned buildings were ever finished, and all the units quickly filled. The two buildings left incomplete had even drawn their own residents, who slept on raw concrete floors and dried their laundry on cords that stretched along the building's open edges. The sparkling tower that the city approved downtown was never finished, either. It too was eventually taken over by squatters, the very people the city had evicted in the first place.

Nothing grew in the sand that circled the apartment buildings. No shade. A few yards from the entrance to Cicely's mother's building, three bony dogs pounced on a dead possum, their small bodies wiggling and jostling. To keep from being nauseated, Cicely turned her head.

The elevator was busted, so they had to walk up to the fifth floor. Kids scampered up and down the stairs around them, slapping one another with tags and screaming. At the landing on the third floor, a boy and girl sat drawing stick figures and houses with chalk on the concrete floor. The air was hot and dense all the way up, but when Cicely's mother turned the key in her door and opened it wide, Cicely felt a blast of chilled air streaming from an AC unit stuck into the corner of a window that looked out over the sandy expanse they had just traversed. Her mother's apartment was small but comfortable, with a red, white, and blue striped rug on the floor and a beige futon in the main room, and a tight, all-white kitchen and bathroom off to the right. The walls were made from cinder blocks, but her mother had painted them in soft alternating colors: yellow, orange, pink. A television sat on a low end table in the corner by the air-conditioner. As soon as she walked inside, Cicely's mother flicked on the TV with a remote. The sound of a toilet flushing, backed by canned laughter, filled the room.

"Have a seat, dear," her mother said, patting the futon. "I'll get us something to drink."

Cicely did as she was told. She heard her mother rummaging in the kitchen. The glow of the TV depressed her, but as she waited she couldn't help but stare. The movie being shown was *Jizz Marquee*, a comedy she recognized from her old work commute.

Her mother returned to the living room, holding a tray on which sat two tall glasses filled with ice and a yellow-brown liquid. "I hope you like a good Arnie Palmer," her mother said, setting down the tray. She handed over one of the cold glasses. "I used to make a big batch of these every Sunday, before we'd go to the beach together. And I'd put it in a big water bottle with ice and just drink from it all afternoon when we'd be there at the beach together." She tapped her glass against Cicely's. "What lovely memories."

"You didn't mention that in your letter."

"I guess it didn't occur to me, honey." Her mother's voice sounded just as she remembered it—maybe a touch weaker, reedier, but otherwise the same.

What did her mother think of her? How had she changed? Probably in ways Cicely herself would never notice. She woke up every day and looked at herself and nothing ever seemed fresh or new, but of course she was different every day, that old self dead and gone. Cicely had grown maybe a couple inches since her mother left, had put on weight, lost it again, put it back on, then figured out some middle ground. Her legs had grown thicker from waiting tables for so many years, and she thought her neck had gotten longer, too, although that seemed impossible, and her hands had grown ugly, kind of gnarled, with deep pits all over them and crosshatching along her wrists, probably another side effect of waiting tables, of handling hazardous cleaners.

Her mother settled into the futon next to Cicely and exhaled. She stared at the TV.

"Mom," putting her hand on her mother's knee, "do I look like you expected me to?"

The question caught her mother off-guard. She turned to

face Cicely; her eyes took a long strut around Cicely's visage. "You look tired, honey."

Cicely scoffed. Had her mother expected a beauty queen? What did she think she had been doing this past decade? Her mother was right, though: she had aged beyond her years. Every now and then, at the dance hall, some man would come with a date she recognized from high school, some girl she had gone to class with or rode the bus next to. The intervening years hadn't touched these girls at all—their tan skin still glowed, their hair still fell in silky waves. It was as if they were kept in a chamber somewhere and only brought out on special occasions to remind everyone else of their ugliness.

"You too," Cicely said. It was true. You could look at someone like her mother and see the years pressing down, the constant struggle to just get up in the morning, the sadness that curled around the edges of the evening, the time of day when everything seemed particularly meaningless. And what was she wearing? The muumuu, the jelly sandals—it was almost as if she had chosen to become an old woman before her time.

The comment annoyed her mother; her expression turned sour. Cicely was glad.

"What kind of work do you do, Mom?"

"I'm at a middle school. I work in the office."

The tea in the Arnold Palmer wasn't fresh and the drink tasted a little funky.

"Isn't today a school day?"

Her mother shook her head. "We've been on a three-day week for a few years now. Rest of the time the libraries just show videos to the kids." She winced. "It's been hard, really hard, to be around kids that age, around the age you were when I moved out." Her head tilted forward and her hand kept smoothing her dress over her knees. She was shaking a little.

"Moved out? You didn't move out." It surprised Cicely how much pleasure her anger gave her. "A roommate moves out. When a couple gets divorced, someone moves out. You didn't move out. You disappeared." Cicely didn't raise her voice, just said these words plainly. Which maybe made them even more vicious.

But her mother didn't break. "You're right, you're right," was all she said.

Someone on TV farted. Laughter broke out. Cicely stood and brushed back the soft window curtain that the sun had stained yellow. On the far side of one of the buildings, on a small plot of cement laid down amid the sand, stood a bent basketball hoop. Three guys were playing a game of twenty-one, which mostly consisted of jacking up contested threes, while a girl stood on the perimeter, clutching a ball of her own. Pricks. For now, the hoop rested in a shadow cast by one of the apartment buildings, but that would change soon. The sun nibbled at the edges of the concrete. How long she had dreamed of being in her mother's home. How little that dream resembled this.

"Does this building have a phone I could use?" Cicely asked, turning from the window.

Her mother slapped something dead with a flyswatter. She pointed to the kitchen. "Cell phone's on the counter there."

Given the humble apartment, it came as a surprise to know her mother could afford a cell phone. She could have called the dance hall any time she wanted.

Cicely had written down the motel's phone number on the inside of her wrist. Taking her mother's phone, she stepped out into the hallway and dialed. Zinnia sounded like she had just woken up, weary and hoarse.

"Hey." It was all Cicely had to say, really. Holding the bright screen of the phone to her ear, she paced the hallway, which made one big loop around the entire floor of the building.

The cinder block walls messed with the cell phone's reception; Cicely could barely hear Zinnia. "I said: where are you calling from?" Zinnia was almost shouting.

Cicely found that if she leaned against the hallway's lone window—a tiny square portal—she could pick up a decent signal. But now that the line was clear, she didn't know what to say. She started to tell the story of her morning, of recognizing her mother, but she ended up just trailing off, letting the story die.

"Are you still there?" Zinnia asked.

"Barely."

"Do you need me to come meet you? I'm sure I can figure out the bus routes if you give me an address."

Sleepiness enveloped Cicely. "No, no."

"Are you spending the night there?"

Getting the words out took so much energy: "She hasn't offered."

"Cicely, come home."

When she reentered the apartment, her mother was reheating pizza in a toaster oven.

"Who'd you call?" her mother asked.

Cicely set the phone back down on the counter. "A friend from home."

Her mother fidgeted, tapping the rim of the sink with her finger and glancing around the kitchen with nervous eyes. "Hope it wasn't long-distance." She said it as a joke, but it came out flat. From the TV in the other room, Cicely heard the grunts of people having sex. "Cicely—" The oven timer cut her off. Shielding her hands with dishcloths, her mother removed two slices from the oven and put them on a paper plate then put in two cold slices and restarted the timer. She seemed glad to have the activity, glad to have a reason to push off whatever conversation she wanted to start. "Go ahead, eat up," she said, pushing the full plate toward Cicely.

To Cicely it felt like it was barely afternoon, but the clock decorated with drawings of reptiles that hung near the fridge told her it was already three o'clock. No wonder she felt exhausted; she had barely eaten all day. She folded a slice of pizza and took a series of gigantic bites. The cheese was gummy, the tomato sauce was loaded with corn syrup, but she didn't mind.

The timer went off again. They took their pizza with them back to the living room, where they could sit.

"Cicely, I need to explain something. I didn't just start

writing you out of the blue." Her mother sounded calm now, as if she had rehearsed this. Cicely braced herself. "That first letter... I had just gotten out of jail when I wrote it, and I felt just lost and desperate and you were the first person I thought of and I couldn't stop myself. Sometimes I wonder if I should have just left you alone." Cicely softened. "I did a dumb thing. I was sneaking into one of the fancy parking garages downtown and stealing whatever I could out of the cars that weren't locked. Just small amounts of cash mostly, but occasionally a cell phone or something I could pawn." Everyone had a scheme of some kind. "And getting locked up was just the lowest feeling I had ever known. So embarrassing, so..." Her head thrashed. "And when I started thinking back about all the stupid things I've done, I kept thinking about your father and getting pregnant and how nothing after that was right except for you, and how with your father, I should have just..." Cicely touched her pizza; it had grown cold. "I should have taken you and run. I know that when I die that's going to be my last memory, leaving the house that morning without you, and when I die it's going to be pure shame inside me." Her mother sucked in huge, deep gulps of air. "And I want you to know that the reason it took me so long to reach out wasn't because I didn't want to, but I was just so ashamed, so ashamed. I thought that if you saw me I would burst into flames."

Everything froze. The outpouring silenced Cicely and had even somehow made the television grow quiet. Cicely could no longer hear anything from outside, no cars passing, no kids yelling, no ball bouncing. There was just her mother and her words.

"I'd like to show you some things, some things I've made over the years." Her mother rummaged in the clutter beneath the futon and pulled out a wide, flat artist's portfolio. From it, she took a stack of fabric circles and began spreading them out on the floor. Cicely's first instinct was to laugh. There were ten embroidered circles, about the size of dinner plates, and each of them featured a face. In the one farthest to the left, the face was that of a young girl, but the stitching was terrible, almost childlike. In the one next to that, the girl was a little older, the stitching a little better, and so on. Looking from left to right, Cicely saw her own face emerge more and more clearly in the fabric, till she came to the tenth one, the most recent, in which the reproduction of her face was scarily accurate, the craftsmanship impeccable. Cicely looked up at her mother, who stood with her hands folded in front of her, watching Cicely to gauge her reaction.

"How did you know what I looked like?"

"Early on, as you can probably tell, I didn't. I just guessed." Her mother sniffled a laugh. "But a couple years ago I came to the dance hall and snuck a photo."

The succession of portraits so stunned Cicely that it took her a moment to respond. "What?" All those nights, all those Mai Tais, all those shitty tips—and she had missed her own mother in the crowd. "You were there? At work?"

Her mother raised her hands as if defending herself: "I had to see you."

"And you said nothing to me. Just took a photo and left."

"Honey, I—"

"How'd you even know I worked there anyway?" This should have been the first question she asked. How had she gotten her address?

"Your father—"

Cicely snarled. "Papa?"

Her mother swayed.

"You spoke with him?"

"He never told you?"

The words tasted like poison.

Her mother mumbled then cleared her throat then spoke deliberately. "Your father and I have been in touch for years."

Cicely needed to go. This whole day had been boiling inside her; now she could no longer contain it. She wanted to break something, wound someone. She regretted coming to Orlando, reading her mother's stupid fucking letters. She wanted to know everything, but didn't want to ask her mother a single thing. Her father, her father. Her rage sharpened when she thought of him, pictured him in that clearing behind their house, on his knees, refusing to apologize, but maybe that was OK, because what would an apology have meant at that point, and as she raged she tried to picture him now, happy to imagine him slaving away on that golf course, sucking in chemicals that were designed to kill with a guy standing behind him lashing him if he slacked off.

Cicely's head spun. "I've got to go."

"Cicely, listen, I …"

Cicely stood and marched to the door. Coming here had been a mistake. Thinking Orlando would be anything but just another place was a mistake. She touched her pockets to make sure she had the money she came with. Her hand on the door handle, she turned to her mother. "What."

"The arrest …"

"What."

"The time in jail … I'm still …"

"What?"

"I still owe them … I …"

Cicely shut the door softly behind her.

42.

Cicely and Zinnia played putt-putt again, at a different course; they had been blacklisted from the other one. Cicely let Zinnia win.

Another day, they took the bus to the water park Cicely had visited as a kid. The entrance fee was now just five bucks. Half the attractions stood broken and wrapped in caution tape. The water smelled sulfurous. They had no bathing suits and so had to rent them. The suits sagged around their bodies and made their hips itchy. As her inner tube slowly lost its air, Cicely floated along the lazy river again and again, just staring up, letting her skin bake in the sun. At the end of the day her arms felt crisp and her legs had broiled red.

At night, Zinnia held her. Cicely would find herself lying there, in bed, half-dreaming, when she'd hear the rustle of sheets and feel the bed quake slightly as Zinnia scooted closer, then she'd feel the warmth of Zinnia's skin against her and and the fabric of her panties pressed against the small of her back. Zinnia would slip her left arm under Cicely's neck, would rest her right hand on Cicely's hip. Feeling hot, Cicely threw off the motel comforter, wrapped her leg around the outside of the sheet, but she never asked Zinnia to back off, never suggested she stay on her side of the bed. Cicely had never known someone to hum while sleeping, but that's what Zinnia did—she'd breathe in, out, in, out, all the while murmuring some tune. Zinnia's soft breath tickled the gentle hairs that grew in waves along Cicely's neck.

After a few more days, they left. Rather than take the bus line all the way back, they got out north of home and walked toward where they had left the van. Neither was surprised to see it still there. What would anyone want with it? Zinnia yanked on the key and it started up with a roar.

Still paranoid, they parked a few blocks from home and crept up to the house through the backyard, watching through the windows for a few minutes before entering as quietly as possible. No one seemed to have visited, no one had rifled through their things. If Anna had sold them out (of course she had sold them out) and if the cops had come (of course they had come), they hadn't shown much interest. In a large cloth bag, Cicely threw whatever would fit—jeans, T-shirts, tank tops, *The Awakening*, cans of black beans, chickpeas, salmon, and the can opener the previous tenant had left in the kitchen drawer. Zinnia moved the van closer to the house and loaded it up with all the music equipment she could: guitars, synthesizers, drums, cymbals, effects pedals, all the gear that had crowded Cicely's bedroom.

They also took pillows and sheets and then drove north, to a park along the bay where they heard there weren't as many dead fish. They slept on cool sand underneath a blanket of mangrove branches.

43.

On election day, Cicely went to find her father. While Cicely and Zinnia had been gone, the planning commission candidates blanketed the city with yard signs, sticking them in medians and along sidewalks, hanging them in storefronts, and wrapping them around telephone poles. They were all red, white, and blue. They all bore stars. The only name Cicely recognized was McCabe. From work, she knew he was the Owner's candidate.

Buses rented for the day and loaded with workers crisscrossed the city, to and from the polling locations that had taken over auditoriums, libraries, and office buildings. Each bus was plastered with the name of the candidate who paid for the rides. McCabe buses seemed to outnumber all others two-to-one. The Owner left nothing to chance.

Driving Zinnia's van, Cicely followed a McCabe bus out east, tracking the road that led to the Owner's golf course. Men in dirty work shirts leaned out the windows of the bus, shouting obscenities at buses with different candidates' names on them as they passed in the other direction. None of the men was her father. Were they like him, though? Conscripted into work on the golf course? What sins had they committed? Cicely didn't know what she would do when she found her father, but inside her lurked rage.

Since she had last seen it, the entrance to the golf course had been cleaned up. The McCabe bus swooped onto the property, the men ducking back inside the windows to avoid being slapped in the face with the branches that met in a canopy above the driveway. Cicely passed by the entrance and pulled off onto the shoulder a little ways up.

Zinnia had told Cicely she wanted to come, but Cicely waved her off. Zinnia didn't push it. Whatever happened, Cicely knew Zinnia would be there when she returned. Where she would go next, what she would do—these were mysteries Cicely now knew she didn't have to figure out on her own. Zinnia had mentioned something about driving north, to Jacksonville, selling the van and all her equipment and using whatever money they had to buy space aboard a ship bound for somewhere, to get out of this country. It sounded too good to be true; it was too good to be true. But at least she and Cicely dreamed together.

First, though: her father. She walked back down the road, toward the entrance to the golf course. As she neared the Wolf Glen sign, the same bus Cicely had followed roared back out onto the road, stocked with more guys who leaned out of the windows, hollering. They chucked empty beer cans at her; the aluminum clunked to the ground near her feet. The polls closed soon. This was probably the bus's final run.

Cicely brushed back branches as she walked up the long driveway, which curved around up to the front of what had once been an impressive clubhouse. Today, though, the roof of the porte-cochère sagged, and holes dotted the tile roof. Every window on the front side had been smashed, and the two cherub sculptures that once guarded the front door had toppled over, faces and wings and wrists snapped off and crumbling on the ground.

The course's first hole had been cleared of the vegetation that swarmed everything else, but no grass had grown back yet. The elevated tee box sloped down to a dogleg fairway that bent to the right, all of it just dirt, sculpted dirt. They had killed every trace of any living thing. Far off, a chemical mist hung in the air, down by where the green and hole and flag stick would one day be. Even from hundreds of feet away, Cicely could smell it. It filled her nostrils with an orange scent, like Tang, or that goopy soap that came out of the dispenser next to the sink at work. It was almost comforting.

A long water hazard traced the left edge of the fairway. The mist had settled into the water, which burbled with orange goo. Was this somehow making its way to the gulf, killing all those fish? Or was it the fertilizer they used to grow everything back, neat and green? Watching the mist drift to and fro, her eyes began to water. The smell went from sweet to nauseating in seconds. Her throat twitched and she bent over, heaving, but there was nothing to come up. She dragged herself over to the front door of the old clubhouse and yanked it open. The windows were busted, but the air inside was still cleaner than outside. She collapsed on a couch that smelled of mildew.

When she recovered, she tore a long strip of fabric from the couch and tied it around her face, covering her nose and mouth. It stank, but it still represented an improvement over the stench that hung outside. She slipped through French doors that led to a veranda out back. From that vantage point, she could see through the dense jungle to what looked like a set of barracks a few hundred yards away. Next to the barracks lay two giant plastic drums filled with a neon orange liquid. Hoses dropped from the tanks and curled up nearby in a small grass clearing. All the grass around the spouts had turned brown and gray.

She pushed her way through the overgrowth, toward the barracks. Inside the dense vegetation, the light around her morphed into darkness, bathing the waxy leaves and sharp bark in a luscious midnight blue. She quickly lost sight of the barracks and the chemical-filled drums, but stumbled ahead in the direction she felt they were in, her hands grasping for holds, her feet catching on roots she couldn't see. Something wasn't right about this place, but it took her a few minutes to pin down what. The golf course, even with all this vegetation, all this green life, was silent. There were no birds singing out, no owls hooting, no mammals crashing through the plants, no frogs croaking, not even any insects chirping or buzzing or screaming. Nothing. Aside from the grass, the weeds, the trees—no life.

But then she did hear something: laughter. And the screech of brakes. The bus must have returned from the polling place; the workers' votes for McCabe had been recorded. Trying to step quietly, Cicely moved in the direction of the chuckles. Pulling open a window in the branches in front of her, she saw a couple dozen men, all in stained and ripped T-shirts, bounding off the bus, which had pulled up along a dirt road that ran up to the barracks from the opposite direction.

"Yo! Come get your beer."

Cicely recognized the voice. The man with the box cutter. And indeed, there he was, leaping from the bottom step of the school bus and walking to the rear to open the bus's emergency hatch. From inside he pulled case after case of beer, tossing them to the ground. The men turned and scampered from the barracks back to the bus, grabbing the paper boxes and hoisting them onto their shoulders. The door to the barracks banged open and more men streamed out. Cicely smelled them from here—a deadly scent of sweat and manure mixed with the chemical burn of the orange mist. The men's skin had turned brown from their days working on the course. Ears, foreheads, bald spots—each had darkened in the sun. But white splotches also touched the men's bodies. Chemical spills? Burns? One man's neck had turned ghostly and pink. Hauling beer back to their quarters, the men looked like primates, even grunted like them. From inside the barracks, Cicely could hear the music from a movie she had seen many times on the bus, a modern classic: *Scrotal Domination*.

She watched the men file inside, already breaking open the cases and tossing beers back and forth. The snap of cans opening popped through the air. She turned her gaze back to the man with the box cutter. He was looking right at her. Shit. She stumbled backward, the branches she had pushed aside slapping back to close off her view.

For a moment, she froze, listening, but he didn't come her way. No footsteps, no shouts. She gently parted the leaves again. He still stood there, staring at her, but his expression had softened. He wore new boots, nice ones that came halfway up his shins, and he had washed his bandanna. Its red fabric almost glowed. Then he smiled. He actually smiled. A small one. No teeth showed. But still. Their eyes locked into each other's. That night in the clearing behind Cicely's house, her father on his knees—it felt so long ago, almost as if it wasn't real, as if it were part of some movie, just something she saw, something a bus driver played for her and everyone else in the middle of a frigid ride. And then the man with the box cutter did something strange: he pulled the box cutter from his belt, held it out in his palm, and nodded toward the barracks. Then he pushed the blade out of its blue plastic shell and tossed the weapon onto the grass in front of him. He turned away, slammed shut the bus's door, and hopped behind the wheel. Before Cicely could understand his gesture, he left.

She stepped out of the bushes. All the men had gone inside, and the space around the barracks had fallen quiet and empty. With the lip of her flip-flop, she nudged the box cutter. It rolled over. The blade was still brown and jagged. She bent over and lifted it. As it had in the clearing that night, it felt heavier than she thought it would. Once again, she saw the blood flowing from her father's neck, felt the pressure that came with pushing the blade into his skin. She had wanted to strike bone.

She walked over to the barracks. High windows ringed the building's curved walls. Cicely pushed a couple empty plastic crates up next to the building and climbed on top. On her tiptoes, she could see into the brightly lit facility. Bunk beds lined the whole floor of the building, the mattresses covered with soiled sheets and dirty laundry. In the far corner sat the TV, around which all the men huddled. Among them, her father. He looked terrible, worse than on his worst days. His cheeks had swollen as if he had been punched and his upper arms and shoulders carried bright red scars, as if he had been whipped. He sat on the floor amid the crowd of men, his legs crossed and his thin blond hair in a tangle atop his burned scalp. He turned his head, and Cicely could see him in profile, could still see a trace of the man in the jeans and white T that her mother had fallen for.

On the television, pundits discussed the day's exit polls. As the program rolled on, one by one, the men, drunk, stumbled outside to piss, holding onto the walls of the barracks to steady themselves as they unzipped their pants.

After what felt like forever, Cicely's father finally stood up, stretched, chucked an empty at the TV, and walked to the door. Cicely hopped down from her perch and looked around, letting her eyes adjust to the dark. Around the corner, on the far end of the building, she heard a door creak open then slam shut. Footsteps crunched out toward a copse, where the tree trunks shined with all the splashed urine. From the corner of the building, Cicely watched as her father, his back to her, tottered toward the trees. When he grew close, he halted and unbuttoned his fly.

Cicely sprinted toward him and pushed him with all her strength. He crumpled way more easily than she imagined he would. His face hit the wet ground. Cicely herself almost tumbled over, but she caught herself with her right hand then stood back up. Her father rolled over to see his attacker. If he was surprised, he didn't look it. His body, tensed for a brawl, grew lax.

"Cicely," he said. Dirt and urine clung to his cheeks. He swatted at his face to clean himself.

Cicely enjoyed standing over him. "I saw Mom."

That did surprise him. He tried to sit up, but Cicely pushed him back with the palm of her hand. He tried to squirm onto his side, but Cicely lowered a knee onto his chest. She could see fear rise in his eyes.

He reached up toward her. "Cicely, please. Take me away from here. Take me away."

Behind her, the barracks door banged open. A man teetered out. He threw a wave at Cicely and her father. "Hey there," he said before tripping on a root and falling over. He lay on the ground moaning.

Cicely's father lunged in the man's direction. "Help!" he shouted, but before he could get out anything more, Cicely fell on him. She pushed down hard on his chest with her knee and twisted her hands around his neck, right below his Adam's apple. His eyes bulged. "Help"—this time little more than a strangled gasp.

The other man hadn't gotten back up. He just lay on the ground, breathing hard.

Cicely ripped off the fabric that covered her nose and mouth and leaned in close to her father's face. The toxic orange scent coated his breath. Frenzy welled up inside her. Her mind felt hot. Her hands shook. This man. This man. She had wasted so much of her life for this man. He had helped create her. But what good was that? Twenty-five years old. Nothing to her name. One friend in this world. She hadn't wasted her life for her father. She had thrown it away for nothing.

Rage made her blubber. A hot mix of tears and drool dripped from her face. Her vision went blurry. Her father had given up. His breath grew slower and slower. He tried to push her away, but his arms went limp and weak. But she didn't want him to die. That thought hit her like ice down the back of her neck. All of a sudden, she saw his face as that of a stranger, just the face of any old man. Wretched, perhaps, but not deserving this.

In an instant, she relaxed her grip and rolled off of him. He turned on his side, gasping and gulping and gripping his throat. As her father drew in more air, he slowly came back to life. Cicely lay on her side, her back to him. Her father scooted over to her and touched her shoulder. She jumped, startled, then turned to look at him. When he spoke, his voice sounded like a croak.

"Cicely," he said, rubbing his neck. "Cicely. I'm sorry. I can't …" He coughed and even vomited a little. He wiped his mouth with the back of his hand. "I'm sorry."

Cicely just stared at him. It was what she had wanted him to say, in the clearing behind their home. But here, outside the barracks, the words meant nothing. They didn't matter at all.

"I don't care enough," she said. Speaking the words made her realize her own thoughts.

Cicely stood up. Leaning down, she offered her father a hand. He took it, and Cicely pulled him onto his feet. She still recognized him underneath the dirt and bruises and blood, still saw the man she used to stay up late playing cards with, the man who would pull her up into his lap and kiss her on her ears. She saw him in there somewhere. She ran a hand through his hair, greasy and clotted.

"Bye, Papa," she said.

She turned away, toward the enormous round tanks that held the toxic orange liquid they were using to kill everything out here. The tanks stood at least twenty feet high. The surface of the orange liquid inside bubbled well above Cicely's head. She touched her hand to the container on the left. It felt warm. Against her palm, the plastic vibrated.

44.

McCabe won, of course, and the plague of dead fish only grew worse. When Cicely and Zinnia went to St. Mark's for the free meal the next Tuesday, Father Bill, in his sermon, said the sickness had been foretold in the Bible and asked for more donations.

Cicely and Zinnia still talked about selling everything and buying a ticket on a boat, but they also felt stuck, unsure what to do next. Rather than getting rid of her gear in one big flush, Zinnia pawned a few pieces here and there so the two could eat. With less equipment cluttering up the rear of the van, they were even able to spread out a blanket in the back and sleep with a roof over their heads.

A thunderstorm swooped in one night and pounded the concrete and beaches, the waves of water flushing out the scum and algae and dead creatures that had accumulated. Through the storm, Cicely and Zinnia lay in the back of the van, holding hands and listening to the sharp rattle of drops on the roof. The trees around them jerked in the screaming wind. The boom of the thunder sounded like the firing of a jet engine.

Early the next morning, Cicely woke. The world seemed fresh and alive. In the wake of the storm, the humidity had dropped drastically, and the air outside the van blew cold and strong. Cicely hunted for a sweater, rarely used. She rubbed her hands together and walked around to warm her legs. Inside, Zinnia snored.

The park where they slept was located on the eastern edge of a narrow bay shaped like a triangle. On the opposite side of the bay, across the green water, a bridge ran between two barrier islands. In happier times, boats stopped here on the weekends and young men and women gathered, floating around on inflated plastic toys, smoking weed and drinking margaritas out of giant convenience store cups, turning from pale white to cooked lobster in the span of an hour or two. When they went home to make love, their genitals glowed white. Now no one came here, not even the rich, but it seemed to Cicely like she could almost see those revelers again, splashing and flirting and killing their days.

She walked around the bay, down to the beach, mechanically, not noticing anything special except that the sun was not hot. There was no one thing in the world she desired.

The water of the gulf stretched out before her, gleaming with the million lights of the sun. The storm had washed all the dead fish and birds and dolphins and turtles out off the beach and into the distant surf. Far out, the bodies floated along the tops of waves. Even farther out, you could still see the storm raging away, dropping sheets of water on the churning gulf. Cicely looked up and down the empty beach. It had not looked so beautiful and clean in months, or years. Although the temperature had dropped, she suddenly felt warm. Piece by piece, she pulled off her clothes, leaving the sweater, the T-shirt, her jeans, her panties, in a bundle on the sand. For the first time in her life she stood naked in the open air. She stepped into the foamy wavelets that spurted up onto the beach and began to walk out. The chill of the water slapped against her stomach and made her shiver, but she held her breath and dunked her red and white body down into the waves with a long, sweeping stroke.

She swam out and out and then out even farther. Her arms and legs grew tired. She thought of her mother and her father and Delanna and Hilda and Anna and Dwayne and the Owner and the man with the box cutter. Exhaustion pressed in upon her. She thought about her goodbye to her father, all the goodbyes she had said over the years. It felt as if the gulf were overpowering her. Treading water, she looked back at the beach, now far away. She thought about Zinnia—to her, now, a sister. But even her: she did not understand. Would she ever? The shore was far behind her; her strength was almost gone. Was it too late? An old terror, but also a longing, flared up inside her. A wave smacked her in the face.

She was far enough out now that she was surrounded by the foam-sputtering bodies of the dead fish that the storm had washed out. Rotting green eyes stared at her. With all her strength, she swam back, gulping air and splashing her arms about. Her legs felt heavy and dead, but she still kicked mightily, and the waves—more forceful than usual, with the storm still out there surging—pushed her forward. With one last forceful stroke, she washed up in the shallows, tiny bits of shells clinging to her elbows and stomach and knees. She flopped over on her back and felt the rush of waves up the inside of her thighs. Her body trembled as she sucked in air.

When she flipped over and propped herself up on her elbows, she saw Zinnia sitting among the dunes, watching her. How long had she been there? Cicely waved; Zinnia waved back. There was still no one else on the beach, no one besides Zinnia to see her as she stood up, nude. She gathered her clothes and trudged up the beach to where Zinnia was sitting. A bewildered smile stuck to Zinnia's face.

"Nice morning for a swim," was all Zinnia said. Maybe she understood more than Cicely knew.

"The first…" Cicely said. She tossed her clothes up onto the dune and then collapsed into the sand. She rolled around till soft grains coated her whole body. The sun was heating up now, and the sand turned crusty and warm in no time. She looked up into Zinnia's face, dark now, with the sun behind it. The rays turned the fringes of Zinnia's silver hair into iridescent ribbons. The world smelled pink and bountiful. Cicely finished her thought: "… in a long, long time."

About the Author

Cooper Levey-Baker is a writer and journalist. His fiction has appeared in the *Sierra Nevada Review* and Burrow Press's *Fantastic Floridas* series, and his journalism has won multiple awards from the Florida Magazine Association and the Florida Society of Professional Journalists.

CPSIA information can be obtained
at www.ICGtesting.com
Printed in the USA
FSHW010307231221
87136FS